DREAMING OF HER COWBOY'S KISS

Cowboy Mountain Christmas
Book 1

JESSIE GUSSMAN

Contents

Acknowledgments

Cover art by Lara Wynter
Editing by Heather Hayden
Narration by Jay Dyess
Author Services by CE Author Assistant

Listen to the unabridged audio for FREE performed by Jay Dyess on the Say with Jay channel on YouTube. Get early access to all of Jay's recordings and listen to Jessie's books before they're available to the general public, plus get daily Bible readings by Jay and bonus scenes by becoming a Say with Jay channel member.

Chapter One

Ruby Barclay fingered the delicate white veil she held in her hand.

In thirty minutes, it would be on her head, and she would be walking down the aisle of her adoptive father's church, getting ready to pledge the rest of her life to Wesley Landry, fellow surgeon and her fiancé for the last five years.

Her stomach curled like strands of spaghetti in a strainer. Her parasympathetic nervous system was obviously on the fritz.

Her hands didn't shake. As a surgeon, she couldn't afford for them to, but her heart was definitely not pumping in the correct rhythm, the electrical impulses interrupted by the adrenaline that flowed freely in her bloodstream.

Her adopted mom, Penny, and her biological sisters had all been helping her get ready, but they'd tromped out just a few minutes ago to make sure everything else was going okay.

She had a few blissful moments to herself.

Maybe not blissful.

Because they were giving her a chance to think that maybe she was about to make a huge mistake.

She and Wesley were not a romantic love match, but they were a match that made sense, and that's what she wanted.

After her parents had been killed in a car accident, she'd vowed to become the best surgeon she could. Maybe a better surgeon would have been able to save their lives.

After all of her training, she was no longer convinced that was true, but it hadn't made her change her mind about what she wanted to do with her life.

She would get the best training she could, work as hard as she could, and do everything she could to save lives and help people.

Wesley came from a long line of surgeons, and he, his dad, and his grandfather, along with several other members of his family, operated in the biggest hospital in Los Angeles.

Marrying Wesley would open doors to her that she could have only dreamed about, and she would be joining the most prestigious family of surgeons in the world.

Together, they would be the most sought-after and skilled team anywhere.

It was most definitely everything she'd ever wanted.

Deep brown eyes set above a long straight nose swirled in her mind.

She blinked and turned to the lone window in the little prayer room at the back of her father's church, looking out at the perfectly landscaped back area, and the covered pavilion where parishioners had dinner on the grounds twice a month, and the playground where the preschool children in the church's daycare happily entertained themselves during the week.

It was bad enough that she was in a white gown. She wasn't going to mess around with little-girl dreams of romance or be swept away by her feelings.

She was analytical. She was strong. She knew exactly what she wanted, and she was going to get it.

Falling in love with a dirt-poor cowboy and being his cook and washerwoman and bearing his kids didn't even begin to realize her full potential. She wasn't going to allow herself to even consider not going through with everything she had planned today.

She turned away from the window and saw the empty brown basket that was supposed to be filled with flower petals.

Maybe she should stand around and wait for someone to come back and help her, but she hadn't been trained to stand around and wait; she'd been trained to take charge and deal with things.

Even flower petals.

Grabbing the basket, she opened the door to the small room in the back of the church and hurried down the hall to the Sunday school room where the florist's assistant had been camped out, unboxing the live rose displays that would be set at every table in the reception hall.

Not wanting to take any more time than necessary and feeling a little exposed in the hall—it wouldn't do for Wesley to see her; she might not be extremely romantic, but no point in pressing her luck and threatening that old adage that it was bad luck to see the bride before the wedding—she didn't bother to knock but yanked the door open and rushed in, twisting so her train, which thankfully wasn't very long, and made it through the door before slamming it behind her.

She knew exactly how fast electrical impulses traveled from the eyes to the brain. She also knew it took the brain slightly longer to process the information and the reactions that came after.

However, she knew before she turned that what she was seeing wasn't what she was supposed to be seeing, and she also knew *this changed everything.*

With the basket held in front of her and her eyes on the floor, she took a breath.

Had she really seen what she thought she saw?

Shuffling sounds came from the worktable, and a familiar voice said, "This isn't what it seems like. Really."

She'd never hidden from the truth. She'd always faced it straight on. She was a fighter.

She jerked her head up and looked her fiancé in the eye. His crisp white shirt was buttoned the whole way up to his throat, and he wore the cummerbund and tie.

His jacket was over the back of the nearest chair, directly underneath his pants and boxers.

The florist's assistant—Ruby wondered if the girl was even out of high school—had managed to untangle herself from Ruby's fiancé and was hunched on the other side of the table, frantically trying to pull on her leggings.

It just took a sweeping glance for Ruby to determine it was *exactly* what it seemed like. She'd had suspicions before, but she'd never walked in and caught Wesley in the act.

The very act.

She didn't need to say anything. He could say all day long that it wasn't what it seemed, but it was.

They both knew it. No question.

The question had become: *what was she going to do about it?*

She'd always scoffed at little-girl romantic dreams, and she'd never thought that she'd wanted those for her own.

She *had* wanted a husband of her own. That wasn't something she ever thought she'd share.

But if she walked away from Wesley now, she wasn't so naïve as to believe that the job she'd been offered in Los Angeles because of their association, being held in high regard, being able to help, being part of not just a power couple but a power family, everything she'd been working toward and thinking about for the last five years would still be hers to grasp.

But if she didn't...she'd be spending the rest of her life wondering when she would be walking in on him and his latest flame.

She didn't want love, had never wanted love, but she had expected fidelity. Loyalty. Respect.

If this was what he did on their wedding day, she could expect even less after they'd been married.

Seconds crawled by while all those thoughts ran through her head.

The florist's assistant had managed to get her leggings on, although as she stood, Ruby kind of suspected they might be on backwards, and they were definitely wrong side out.

At least she was covered.

Wesley had struggled into his boxers, but now he stood, hands at his sides, not trying to insult her intelligence anymore, as though he knew that he wasn't going to be able to bluff her.

She had a choice to make.

He watched her with intelligent eyes, calmly. He was a skilled surgeon after all and was not ruled by his emotions either.

He was ruled by something else apparently.

Did she want to be married to a man like that?

A negative answer to that question would change the trajectory of her life.

It probably hadn't even been a minute that she'd stood there—since she'd walked in—but sometimes life changed just that fast.

Her experiences as a trauma surgeon had taught her that.

The door behind her burst open, and the florist said, "Oh! Ruby. I thought I saw you come in here..."

She'd gotten that much of her sentence out before her eyes had taken in what the room, and her brain, had told her mouth.

Working.

A few more seconds and the florist knew exactly what had been going on in this room before Ruby stepped in.

Since it was her wedding day, Ruby should be feeling more pain than what she was. Maybe that would come later, or maybe it wouldn't come at all.

She hadn't been in love with Wesley. But she'd thought of love as more of an action and not those girly-girl feelings she never allowed herself the luxury of feeling.

Right now, she was more embarrassed than anything. If Wesley was going to cheat on her, the least he could do was do it without getting caught.

The way he'd been doing it for the last five years.

Was this what she wanted the rest of her life to be? Never knowing when she was going to walk in on her husband messing around with whatever woman was cute and willing?

They'd decided they weren't having children.

In the back of her head, she'd always thought they could change that decision if they wanted to.

She wasn't bringing children into a marriage like that. She wanted her children to have the example of a marriage like her birth parents had. Like Penny and Race.

"Thank you, Ginny," she said, her tone cultured and cool. "The flowers are beautiful." She turned with a small smile, worthy of an ice princess. "Obviously, from what you can see in here, I won't be enjoying them any longer. If Wesley doesn't pay your bill, please send it to me. I'll make sure it gets paid."

Maybe that last bit was a little petty, but she could see Wesley saying since he didn't use the flowers, he shouldn't have to pay for them.

Turning regally, as regally as she could under the circumstances, Ruby lifted the front of her dress and stepped out of the room, starting off down the hall at a sedate, prideful pace.

But as soon as she turned the corner, she started walking faster, and by the time she reached the steps to the basement, she was running. Her only thought: *to get out of there.*

She needed to go somewhere where she could be alone.

Chapter Two

Ethan Shuff stood in the back of the church with his adopted dad, Race Steiner, and tugged at the collar of his stiff white shirt.

He'd worn jeans and flannel to weddings before, more than he cared to count, because he never enjoyed them, no matter how dressed down he was allowed to be, but this wasn't exactly that kind of wedding.

"It's almost time for the music to start," Race said beside him, looking at his watch and clasping his hands behind his back. His eyes surveyed the sanctuary, which was filled to capacity.

"I should go sit down," Ethan said.

His brothers were all up near the front, sitting in a row together. Ruby's fiancé had wanted his own groomsmen, and she hadn't had any of her brothers participating, although both of her sisters were in the bridal party.

Ethan figured she probably didn't consider him a brother.

He certainly didn't consider her a sister. She'd only lived with Race and Penny a few months before she'd graduated and gone off to college.

He hadn't ever considered her a sister.

"Wait until it's almost time for the bridal party to start walking up the aisle." Race glanced over at Ethan. "Please."

Ethan almost smiled, because there hadn't been too many times in his life he'd seen his dad nervous. That, if nothing else, made today different.

He hadn't told Race that he didn't want to come, had almost just not shown up, but he knew it would hurt his parents' feelings, and his siblings wouldn't understand, so he'd sucked it up, pulled out clothes he hadn't worn in years, and gone to watch the woman he'd loved for over a decade and a half pledge her life to another man.

Some well-dressed guests that Ethan didn't recognize walked by them, and he nodded his head as they lifted their chins to acknowledge him.

Race greeted them, and Ethan moved his eyes across the perfectly and tastefully decorated sanctuary.

Ruby's wedding.

This was not how he had pictured it in his head.

He'd known, almost from the beginning, that she would never be his.

That hadn't kept him from fighting for her. It hadn't kept him from hoping and dreaming either.

He'd always made sure he was around when she was visiting, and he thought she considered him a friend.

He doubted she had any idea he wanted to be more. He hadn't pushed; knowing she wanted to be a doctor—a surgeon—and knowing she wouldn't want her dream derailed, he'd stood back.

He'd stood back too long, though. He figured he'd make his move, maybe, once she was done with residency, but she brought home a fiancé five years ago, and that had pretty much ended his dream.

Beside him, Race's hands came unclasped from behind him, and he shifted, agitated.

In a low voice, Race said, "I left my sermon notes downstairs in the kitchen when I stopped to help Penny carry some things in from her car in the back lot. I know I put them on the counter, but I never picked them back up." He rubbed his hands together. "I'm going to run down and grab them, if anyone wants to know where I am."

Race started to walk away, but Ethan put a hand on his arm. "I'll go get it. You stand here. People are more likely to want to talk to you than me."

Race knew a few of the older doctors who had flown in from California. It had been fifteen years or more since he'd quit surgery at the height of his career to become a pastor, but people still remembered him.

"Thanks." Race seemed to relax. "I know they're on the counter. I can see me setting them there plain as day. Your mother distracted me." He winked. "We can blame it on her."

"I know, Dad. She's got broad shoulders. She can take it."

Race laughed and clapped Ethan on the shoulder. "Love you, boy. Even if you do favor your mother."

Ethan laughed. Race and Penny had been married when they were younger and gotten divorced. It seemed like they'd gotten wiser though, and the second time around, they'd had a great marriage.

Ethan had watched them, not with envy exactly, but with the desire to have a marriage with as much fun as what they did.

Ruby was probably too serious and driven to have a good marriage like that, but somehow his heart hadn't gotten the memo, and she was the only one he'd ever wanted.

After today, he needed to figure out a way to get her out of his mind, because he wouldn't covet another man's wife.

He left the sanctuary and went down the short hall to the steps, heading down and striding to the kitchen, which was pretty much deserted except for a little girl who looked like she might have been coming out of the restroom and a teenager who he guessed was late and coming in the back way.

Exactly what he would have been doing if he could get away with it, only he wasn't a teenager anymore.

Race's sermon notes were exactly where Race had said they would be, and Ethan picked them up. He'd never felt called to be a preacher, but he loved helping his adopted dad with church activities.

It wasn't that he was afraid to get up in front of people, because he could do that. It was just taking care of a church was a big responsibility, and his heart had always been in farming.

But he'd found a way to use that love to reach out to underprivileged kids, and for the last five years, he'd been expanding and growing the idea that had first come to him when he'd talked to his dad just a couple of months after Ruby had announced her engagement.

He supposed he'd been depressed, and Race had searched him out because he was concerned about him.

Ethan had never told him what the real cause of any unease that he had was, which was just as good, because Race and he had come up with a really good idea between the two of them, and it was satisfying work.

He fingered the Bible, with the paper of sermon notes sticking out, and looked out the window at the cars in the parking lot. His motorcycle was parked in the back. He'd always figured he'd trade it in when he got married.

He did have a classic in his barn. Not exactly a family car. Sentimental value only.

He'd never need anything more, not without a wife and family.

Shoving those depressing thoughts aside and determined that he wasn't going to pine over her for the rest of his life, he strode with perfect, purposeful steps out of the kitchen and around the corner to the stairs.

Seemed like he wasn't the only one going somewhere on purpose, as a flurry of white came barreling toward him.

Admittedly, he had plenty of time to get out of the way. But once he figured out what, or who, exactly, was coming toward him, he chose not to.

Two seconds later, she barreled straight into him.

Prepared, he staggered back a few steps, putting his arms around her to steady them both.

"Let go. I need to leave. Let me go." Her voice was low and urgent, and she hadn't looked at him yet. She probably hadn't realized yet exactly who she'd run into.

She struggled, still not looking up.

"Ruby," he said, his hands finding her shoulders. "What is it?"

Cold feet?

He could only hope. Obviously, she was leaving. Unless she had left something down here, too. But surely she would have sent Penny or one of her sisters down to get it.

There were restrooms upstairs, but maybe they were full. Maybe she was rushing down here because she couldn't wait in line.

He almost loosened his grip with that thought, but he waited.

"I need to leave. I need to go. Let me out."

"What happened? Have you changed your mind?" Maybe that was the obvious question, or maybe the answer to that question was obvious, but Ethan just couldn't believe that Ruby had spent five years preparing for something and was going to run away at the last minute.

That wasn't the Ruby he knew.

"Ethan?" She stopped struggling and looked up. After two seconds of searching his eyes, she slumped in his arms and laid her forehead on his shoulder.

This wasn't the Ruby he knew either. She didn't lean on people.

He'd seen her several times during medical school and residency. Different times when she'd called Race, asked for advice, and admitted that she was feeling overwhelmed and exhausted.

At least a dozen times, Ethan had been the one to drive, first to New England, where she'd gone to medical school, and then to Chicago, where she spent her residency, but even then, she'd never been like this. Willing to just lie in his arms.

He'd honestly take her any way he could get her. As long as she didn't have another man's ring on her finger.

"I can't do it. I thought I could. But I can't."

"You changed your mind?" He found that so hard to believe.

Her face came up, and for the first time since he'd known her, there was no confident, almost prideful look. She looked like a lost little girl, which was odd, since she was a doctor and a successful surgeon and about to marry and move to California. Then, from what he understood, fall into the lap of the most powerful and famous medical family in the country.

"Yes. I changed my mind." Her words still had some pride in them, but her eyes were cast down, and her spine slumped.

"Ruby. I know you better than that." Something happened.

"I would prefer people not know exactly what happened."

"Am I relegated to the reams of 'people' in your life?"

His question didn't even get a lip twitch out of her.

"I walked in on Wesley and the florist's assistant. They weren't talking about flowers. They weren't talking at all."

That had been his impression of Wesley the first time he'd seen him. An arrogant, cocky, favored son, who had never been told "no." Being told "no" helped develop character.

Character was something Wesley didn't have much of.

"You have a car?" He thought she'd arrived this morning in a vehicle with her sisters and her mom. He wasn't a member of the bridal party, but there was a sports car outside decorated with "Just Married" signs and crepe paper. He was pretty sure that sporty little low-slung thing wasn't Ruby's.

Her eyes widened, and her hand came up to her cheek, cupping it. "I hadn't thought of that." She sighed, irritated. "He's taken my pride *and* my brain. How did I not remember that I didn't even have a vehicle here?"

"I've got my bike. I'll take you wherever you want to go."

"I don't even know where I want to go. Just out of here."

There were sounds coming from the top of the steps, and her eyes opened wide. She gripped his hand.

"Please. Take me away. Somewhere. Anywhere. I don't care, just get me out of here. I'm going to have to call everyone and cancel, but I don't want to do it in front of everyone, give me at least the screen of the phone before I have to make those calls."

She didn't need to ask him twice. He'd never told her he'd do anything for her, but he would.

He grabbed her hand. "Come on. I'll take you somewhere you can think, and then you can decide what you're gonna do."

He didn't ask her if she was sure. He didn't want to give her that option. Not the option to change her mind. He'd never gotten the impression, over the holidays and occasional summer weekends that he'd spent around Wesley, that Ruby and Wesley were madly in love with each other. Still, even if it wasn't a huge love match, surely she wanted fidelity and loyalty.

Surely.

They'd gone around the corner before footsteps started down the steps, and they broke into a jog.

"Our parents are going to be surprised," he said as she ran by his side.

"They won't be disappointed in me. Not when I tell them what Wesley was doing. If it gets out, there are going to be people who won't understand, who will think I should have just stayed with him. But not our parents." She had her wedding dress gathered in both hands and matched her stride to his.

"You're right about that."

They ran out the back door and jogged to his bike, getting on as she adjusted her dress, tucking it under her.

"That thing will be ruined."

"I don't think anybody else will want to wear it anyway. Not after what happened today." If she were upset about the cost, she didn't say.

He wanted to shoot a quick text off to Race, at least, and let him know what was going on. But it was only a short ride to his ranch, maybe twenty minutes. He didn't want to waste time.

"Are you sure about this?" he felt compelled to ask, out of unselfishness, he supposed, because he certainly didn't want her to second-guess herself.

"Yes," she said with complete assurance. "Let's get out of here."

She wrapped her arms around his waist, and he couldn't stop the shudder that went through him. She had to have noticed, but he didn't sit around and give her time to say anything. He started the bike, twisted his right hand, and carefully let out the clutch, motoring out of his stall, twisting around a couple of latecomers who had parked along the edge, and pulling out into the drive.

As they went by, Wesley opened the basement door and put his head out.

"You can't do this to me!" he screamed after them. "Get back here."

"Keep going," Ruby said in his ear.

Ethan grinned. "I was hoping you'd say that."

"And don't stop. Don't stop for anything." Ruby's voice had grown stronger, and some of the steel and pride that had always been in it had come back.

She was making the right decision. Now, he just had to figure out how to get her to notice him.

Chapter Three

What had she done?

Ruby held tight to the solid waist in front of her as Ethan gunned the motor and they raced down the highway.

The hair that her sisters, Journee and Blakely, had taken so long to fix that morning snapped around her face. Completely ruined.

Her dress was hopelessly wrinkled under her butt. She had pretty much made a decision, and the bridges were all burning behind her.

She never made decisions with her emotions. Never.

She hadn't gotten to where she was in life by getting angry and running off. Which is basically what she'd done. Angry and hurt.

Her pride was hurt anyway.

Her heart might be a little relieved.

Her eyes slid to the strong lines of the tan neck in front of her. Her heart actually was pretty happy.

Was it divine intervention that had the cowboy she spent her life dreaming about coming up the stairs as she'd been going down?

Sure, he'd haunted her dreams.

Not haunted them, drove them.

Since her parents had died, no one, not even her adoptive parents, had supported her like Ethan had.

Penny and Race didn't even know about some of the things he'd done.

She'd been determined to keep him at arm's length, because he wasn't what she wanted in her life. Even now, he really wasn't what she wanted.

Except he was.

He'd come and visited her at medical school six times, not that she was counting. And he'd visited her during her residency just as many.

Somehow, when she called home, completely overwhelmed and unsure if she was going to make it or drop out, her parents had talked her down, and then Ethan had shown up.

And yet, she'd never even been to the farm that he bought, what was it, eight years ago?

She'd been too busy working toward her own dreams and hadn't cared about his.

Hadn't *allowed* herself to care about his.

And yet, it hadn't stopped him from coming to her anytime she needed him.

Over the years they'd known each other, he'd done everything she needed, and look at them now. He was still rescuing her.

Maybe it was a funny thing to think about on the wild motorcycle ride away from the wedding that she was supposed to be participating in.

She should be thinking about Wesley, and angry at what he'd done, and trying to figure out the logistics of shutting everything down and apologizing to her guests...although, really? Was it her job to apologize to her guests for Wesley?

Whatever, none of that was on her mind.

She couldn't stop thinking that Ethan had always been there for her. Not in a loud or bold way.

Just, when she needed it, he slipped into her life. Cheered her up, took her out, made her sleep, fed her, whatever she needed, and then slipped back out.

And yet, what had she ever done for him?

She half expected him to take her to Race and Penny's house. That's kind of where she thought she'd go. Her clothes were all in Wesley's car.

Clothes! What was she going to wear?

Did it matter? She could cut the train off the dress and wear it for a while. Might as well get something out of the money she'd spent on it.

Ethan blew by the turnoff for Race and Penny's house, and she assumed he was taking her to his ranch. That was fine by her. Over the years, they'd talked about how nice it was and how private. It would be the perfect place for her to hang out for a night and figure out what in the world she was going to do.

The sun shone on her face, and she lifted it, enjoying the beautiful June day, deep blue sky, the Arkansas Ozarks in the background, and an honorable man taking her away from what probably was the worst situation of her life.

But it wasn't life and death. Not like she saw every day at her job. And somehow, she just couldn't get that upset about it.

The road wound around, houses becoming more and more scarce before they disappeared altogether, leaving nothing but fields, rolling hills, and the occasional herd of cows until he turned off on a dirt road.

He slowed way down, and as a trauma surgeon, she was kind of happy about that. She'd seen some pretty messed-up people from motorcycle accidents go through the ER.

She hadn't been thinking about that when she climbed on with him. She really wasn't too worried about it now. Somehow, Ethan's quiet confidence reassured her that she was fine, leaving her to focus on the glorious day around her.

They turned down yet another dirt road, a lane that should be in a Norman Rockwell painting, as they went what seemed like further and further away from civilization.

They had to have spent at least ten minutes on unpaved roads before the open fields peeled back on each side of them, and they motored down through a tree-lined drive with split rail fencing on both sides and a placid herd of cows grazing on the left. On the right, she could look down the hill and see glimpses of water. A river? Or a large creek.

She wasn't sure where they were anymore. Sad, since she had grown up in this part of Arkansas.

A huge old barn dominated the spread before them when they came out of the tree line, with a smaller white-sided house that looked like an old farmhouse painting that would be hung up in a museum somewhere. Various outbuildings were scattered around, and flowers and bushes bloomed in profusion.

She wouldn't have thought of Ethan as someone who would have flowers blooming all around his house, but in hindsight, she could see him carefully tending the plants in his yard in the evening.

She had a little more trouble picturing him relaxing in the typical ways everyone she knew did—hanging out at a bar, hooking up. Or, like several doctors she knew, playing in a cover band on their days off. Or the more typical hanging out in front of the TV or surfing the net.

None of that seemed like Ethan.

Then she realized she didn't really know what he might do in his spare time.

He pulled around the side of the house, kicked the stand down, and settled the bike before turning it off. Both legs were braced on either side, and he didn't turn around.

They just were still, looking out over the view.

The house sat on a rise, and rolling hills stretched off in the distance, no houses in sight.

"It's beautiful back here," she said softly, feeling like she needed to talk when he hadn't.

All the times he'd rescued her, she knew he wasn't a big talker. Of course, she'd always been the one with the problem. He'd asked questions to draw her out, and she usually ended up holding up both ends of their conversations.

He looked over his shoulder and met her eyes. "I think so."

Those dark eyes. Swirled like sandstone around an old fireplace. Rich and layered and deep. She knew nothing of what was in the depths. Although somehow, when he was looking at her, it made her shiver on the inside and think that maybe he wasn't really talking about the view. As she had been.

"I'm impressed by the blooming flowers," she said.

His eyes held hers for just a second more before he looked around and nodded.

The only other vehicle in sight was a beat-up old farm truck, although she supposed there could be anything parked in the barn. There was a shed beside it which could probably hold vehicles too, as well as the huge pole building across the driveway.

Now that she was here, and they were stopped, she felt a little awkward, which was weird because she never felt awkward around Ethan.

She'd never gotten on board with the idea that he was her brother, either. He hadn't officially been adopted.

People don't dream about their brothers.

"Are you okay?" he asked, his words flowing out away from them, but as though he couldn't keep from using his eyes to try to figure out if her words were going to be true, he looked back.

"I'm fine. I'm glad it happened before I said 'I do.' I feel like I dodged a bullet. But this really messes up everything I had planned for my future."

He straightened and pulled a leg over the bike carefully so as not to kick her.

"Come on. We'll make some lemonade, and sit on the porch, and make the phone calls we need to in order to get this straightened out. Our parents are probably going crazy."

He held a hand out for her. She stared at it. Her colleagues all had smooth white hands, almost delicate, slender fingers. Their hands were their income, their life's work, where the healing took place.

They were tools to be guarded, protected, babied even. Some surgeons had their hands insured. Maybe like concert pianists or other top-tier musicians.

If anything happened to her hands, she would not be able to make a living.

The hand he held out to her was almost the exact opposite in every way of what hers were.

Rough. Brown. Calloused and scarred. His were the hands of the people she worked *on*. Not the people she worked *with*.

And yet, those hands had been soft and kind as they'd rubbed her back and urged her to rest. As they'd done her laundry and cleaned, first her dorm, then her apartment, while she slept. As they had cooked for her and taken care of her, fed her and stroked her brow the year she'd had the flu and crashed on Race and Penny's couch.

Ethan had been the one to sit up with her at night and to take off work to be with her during the day.

She hadn't thought too much about it at the time, because he was the one who wasn't busy in the winter, as his ranch work slowed down.

She stared at his hand a second and a half too long, which felt like an eternity. But it didn't move, like it was up to her to accept or reject it. He wasn't going to rescind his offer just because it took her a little while to make up her mind.

She slid her fingers into his, slender and cool, perfectly manicured, which was slightly unusual, but thanks to the wedding, her nails were short and serviceable but also shiny perfection.

"I know this wasn't what you were planning on doing tonight."

"Plans change," she said briskly, standing and swinging her leg over his bike, needing his steadying hand as her gown got caught and she unhooked it, hopping on one foot and wishing she'd chosen to wear flats instead of high, spiky heels, which she wasn't used to.

Wesley liked heels.

He grunted; whether it was at her, or whether he hadn't expected her to work so hard over her balance, she wasn't sure.

"I'm sorry. Not used to having all this stuff around me." She slapped at her gown, making it fall back around her legs, covering her completely. "All my clothes are packed in Wesley's car. I'm sure he probably won't think about taking them out before he drives away. I have stuff from my apartment in Chicago. I was cleaning it out, because I was getting ready to move to LA."

"You're probably about my height. You might have to roll my cuffs up, but you'll fit my jeans."

His voice was low and slow, but his words made her eyes shoot toward his. And blink. She hadn't considered that, but he was probably right. He was a couple inches taller than she was, but they were both slender.

She'd been engaged to Wesley for five years, and she'd never put a single piece of his clothing on.

That helped her make up her mind. "I'll take you up on that. Anything's better than this crazy dress."

"Come on." He tugged on her hand. Maybe it was her job to pull her hand away, but he didn't drop it, and she didn't pull, and they walked up the stone sidewalk to his back porch with their hands linked.

He opened the door for her. She bunched her dress together to get it through the doorway, and his two shaggy mutts came running out.

She supposed, somewhere in the recesses of her brain, she'd heard the barking.

He kept his elbow holding the door open but dropped on one knee to pet the two heads.

She stopped.

"Are you going to introduce me to your family?" she asked with an eyebrow raised. She'd never had time for pets. Her last was a fish. She even killed houseplants because she just didn't remember to water them or didn't have the energy after thirty-six-hour shifts.

But she did know that some people really put a lot of store in their animals, especially if they didn't have children.

She supposed she got cynical, and maybe a little hard, because she faced death every day in the OR, and a pet was just one more thing to get attached to. Maybe it didn't seem like that life was nearly as important as a human life.

But it was her opinion.

Ethan seemed pretty enamored with his dogs as they wiggled around him and licked his face.

She dropped to her knee. Why not? It wasn't like she was ever going to wear this dress again. She held her hands out for the little black noses to sniff.

"This is Crimson. And this is Slipper," Ethan said shortly, pointing to each dog, his head down, not looking at her.

They sniffed her hands, then shoved their noses at her, their bodies wiggling, trying to get closer.

"They're friendly." And he chose interesting names. She wondered...

"Yeah, they love everybody. Not really good watchdogs, but that's okay. I'm always gonna have people running around here, and I wouldn't want to have a dog I have to watch because I was afraid it would bite someone."

"You're so far out you really need a watchdog. Someone could sneak up on you and take everything you have."

"I guess they're welcome to it, then."

That was a different kind of attitude, as well.

"What kind of dogs are they?" she asked, unsure how to answer that last comment.

"I don't know. Just a bunch of different things, I guess. I had a friend whose buddy had a litter of pups, and he got these two, but his wife couldn't handle them, and he was looking to give them away. I took them both. They're high energy, but they've settled down over the years."

"So they're not puppies?" She knew nothing about dogs. Maybe that was a dumb question.

At his laugh, she was convinced it was.

"No. I got the dogs not long after I got the ranch. They're probably eight or so. I didn't really keep track."

She nodded.

His hands, so big and brown and strong, handled the dogs with a gentle care that captivated her. She had to pull her gaze away, settling it on an orange tabby cat that wove in and out of her legs. She scratched it between the ears and could feel its body vibrating with its purring.

"That's Mr. Rogers," Ethan said.

"Sweet kitty," she said, as Mr. Rogers pushed into her hand, loving the attention. She could feel her stress draining away. There was something soothing about petting an animal and something even better about the unconditional love they showed.

The dogs wiggled around, pushing the cat away. The dogs looked so similar to each other.

"How do you tell them apart?"

"Crimson's just a little bigger, and she has more white on her." His long brown finger pointed out the white along Crimson's belly, legs, and face. "Slipper has white paws in the front."

"That's how she got her name then?"

"Not really. But I guess it works if you want to think about it that way."

"Do you have a lot of animals here on the farm?"

"The usual. Slipper and Crimson. Mr. Rogers and a few other barn cats that aren't as friendly. A herd of beef cattle and a hog behind the barn that should have babies sometime this month." He didn't look at her when he said it, and he straightened before she could say anything more.

"I'm sure you want to get out of that thing," he said, looking at her dress and completely changing the subject from the dogs' names.

It was funny how one could put Ruby and Slipper together, and Crimson and Ruby were similar. But maybe she was just being egotistical, needing everything to relate to her.

She didn't like to think of herself as selfish, but when it came to Ethan, she kinda felt she had been.

"You're right. It will be nice to put this behind me."

She hesitated. There was a line of pearl buttons down the back of her dress, and it was going to take forever and a day to unhook them all, if she even could. She had never put the dress on by herself, not any of the times when she'd tried it on and not today.

"Just go straight through the mudroom and into the kitchen." Ethan spoke from behind her as the dogs ran outside, and he shut the door.

"Don't you have them in a pen or something?"

"No. They stick around. Plus, everything you can see from the house, I own. So even if they didn't stay close, they're welcome to roam."

She opened the door and walked through a small room into a big country kitchen. It wasn't any dirtier than her apartment had been and a lot cleaner than it usually was.

There were a couple coffee cups in the sink and two dirty plates. The counters were wiped off, although there was a package of spaghetti noodles and a can of sauce sitting out. A tea towel lay on the counter like he'd thrown it down after drying his hands, and there were a couple of crumbs at the table like maybe he'd eaten breakfast and not wiped it.

Regardless, the floor looked like it'd been swept within the last week, and she'd seen a lot of places that were much worse off.

"I'm impressed. Looks pretty clean in here. More so even than my apartment."

"Nobody else is going to do it, and I don't like living in the mess."

"You don't have a housekeeper?" She turned around to look at him, because she was kind of kidding. But he didn't smile. He'd always been very serious.

"No, although Natalie will be here next week cooking."

She managed to keep her mouth closed, but her brows shot up. "Natalie?"

"We went by her place—the last house we went past. She rents that small house on the farm that borders mine down by the river."

He didn't seem inclined to elaborate, and she didn't ask any more questions. It was the first time she'd ever thought that Ethan might have a girl. He'd never mentioned anyone, never brought anyone with him on family weekends or for the holidays when she'd been around. He was alone at the wedding today.

Ethan had always struck her as a loner.

"You go through those doors, down the hall, up the steps right there. My room's the first door on the right. Help yourself to whatever you can find in the dressers."

He opened the refrigerator door and pulled out a glass container with cut-up lemons swirling in it. She had to admit to being impressed. She certainly didn't have homemade lemonade in her refrigerator to offer any guests that might happen to show up.

"Are you hungry?" He nodded at the sauce and noodles on the counter. "I was going to get real fancy tonight and make spaghetti."

"I'm not." Her stomach hadn't settled, although her body felt calmer.

He pulled his phone out and looked at it before saying, "That's Dad. If you don't mind, I'll let him know what's going on."

"Please do. I'll call Mom as soon as I'm changed." She pulled her bottom lip in and chewed on it for a couple of seconds, not really wanting to do what she knew she needed to. "I, uh, I really hate to ask this of you, but...I don't think I can get out of the dress by myself. I can probably get all but the very middle buttons..."

His thumbs had been going over the keypad on his phone, but somewhere in the middle of her words, they stopped. Several seconds ticked by.

His eyes, dark and hooded, narrowed as they looked at her. Something swirled in them that almost made her want to take a step back. She held her ground.

His words came out slow. "You want me to unbutton your dress?"

She started to nod her head but scolded herself for being silly.

"Yes." Her voice came out with confidence. It wasn't her fault she couldn't get out of her dress. "Unless you have a pair of scissors, and then I'll just cut right down the front, and I won't have to worry about the buttons."

She hadn't meant to be funny, but his lips twitched.

Without moving from where he was standing, without taking his eyes off her, he reached over and pulled out a drawer.

Glancing down, he grabbed something out, closed it, and handed her a pair of scissors, handle first.

"If you don't have a preference, I do," he said, and she wasn't sure what to make of that.

Her hand reached out for the scissors without conscious thought. But she stopped just short of touching them.

"I do have a preference." She turned her back on him. "I don't know for sure that your clothes are going to work. If I cut this dress off, and they don't, I'll have to wear a towel on the motorcycle ride home."

He snorted. "Isn't it your job to cut and sew? Surely you could make something wearable out of all that material."

She pursed her lips. "I could also take the top five layers of your skin off and make something that would be suitable as well. But I won't...*if* you unbutton the middle buttons of my dress." She spoke crisply, although still joking, but there'd been some kind of undercurrent in his words, and she wasn't sure exactly what he was driving at. Or why he would prefer her to cut her dress rather than him unbuttoning what amounted to probably five buttons that she couldn't reach.

He hadn't started, although she felt his breath waving along the fine hairs of her neck. Apparently not everything had fallen out of her upswept hairdo. She probably looked like a riot happened on her head. And here she was giving him sass about her dress. He was probably laughing at her. *That* was the undercurrent.

"I'm waiting," she said, because she wasn't very good at waiting, and he hadn't even started, and it was making her nervous. What was the problem?

Chapter Four

Ethan stared at the white row of shiny pearl buttons in front of him. Tiny little things that clasped the material around Ruby and covered the skin he'd never seen.

There had been more than one time in his life where he dreamed about Ruby and her wedding dress and him taking it off. Never anything he actually thought would happen.

Certainly not like this. The dress wasn't meant for him, she didn't wear his ring, they hadn't said vows to each other, yet there she stood in her dress, calmly asking him to take it off and having no idea what those words and the idea of that action did to him.

How they mimicked something he'd wanted for so long and yet still wasn't getting.

It was irony probably, although he couldn't say he appreciated it.

The dress dipped into a V in the back, showing lots of flawless white skin along with her slender neck and the fine hairs at the nape of it as they floated around, stirred by his breath.

Definitely it was a fantasy. Or maybe it was making a mockery of his fantasy.

"Fine," she said, irritation plain in her voice. "I can cut the dang dress if you want me to. I don't see what your problem is. It's not like I'm asking you to slit your throat, although I could fix that, too, if necessary."

She crossed her arms over her chest but didn't move, although he wished she would.

Maybe he should tell her what the problem was. Maybe he should say she hadn't put that dress on intending for him to help her take it off.

Or that he'd wished for years that he would have the honor of having her dress like this for him and that he didn't want to unbutton her dress without touching his lips to the sensitive spot at the nape of her neck, and being so close to the smooth skin without being able to run his fingers over it was agony.

No. That probably wouldn't go over so well.

Ruby was a lot of things, but romantic wasn't one of them.

Funny, because people would not look at him and think romance. He supposed, in a way, they'd be right. Because his thoughts only ever ran in that direction with Ruby. He'd just never been interested in anyone else.

She smelled like roses but with an underlying steel and determination that had always been part of her scent.

He looked at his hands. He could do it. He would. She couldn't ask him to do anything that he wouldn't do to the best of his ability.

Anything.

He couldn't let her know it though. He didn't want her to realize, because then she'd feel compelled to tell him that they would never work out.

That she wasn't meant to be a farmer's wife.

That she wouldn't be happy on the farm, cooking and cleaning and raising a bunch of kids and helping out with whatever he needed outside.

She hadn't spent the last fifteen years of her life working and studying and driving herself almost into the ground just to give it all up.

Color him selfish, because he didn't want anything less.

She didn't need to tell him it wouldn't work. He already knew it.

His hands came up, and his thumbs, big and clumsy, worked like they were swollen elbows instead of the most dexterous part of his body.

"I guess this wasn't something the designers of the dress meant to be easy and quick."

He supposed, if they were in a hotel room together or a honeymoon suite somewhere—although he would prefer to just come home, for him that would be the best honeymoon—he supposed being forced to remove the dress slowly would be a really good thing in a lot of ways he didn't even want to think about.

It wasn't supposed to be done in the kitchen of some dude she didn't marry, with her holding a pair of scissors and threatening to cut it off.

She sighed, the hand with the scissors dropping to her side. "Everything about this dress is for looks, nothing is practical. I guess I thought for one day in my life, I could be whimsical. But I should have known better. Because that's not me, and it just ended up biting me, over and over." She sounded bitter and frustrated, and he felt bad for giving her a hard time, no matter how hard what she'd asked him to do was, because she'd just been jilted at the altar, and he hated any pain that might be causing her.

"I'm doing the best I can. Sorry."

Her shoulder lifted in a shrug, and he bit back a word of frustration as the stupid button slipped out of his clumsy fingers yet again without coming unhooked.

"Hold tight to the scissors, because right now if I see them, I can guarantee I'm gonna try to grab them right out of your hand."

One slim shoulder lifted.

He closed his eyes.

"Maybe that's for the best. It might actually be cathartic for me to cut the stupid thing up. Are you sure your clothes will fit me?"

No. He wasn't.

"They might be a little tight around the hips, but it's kind of hard for me to judge your size with this thing on." He was just going by what she looked like the last time he saw her, which should've been last night at the rehearsal dinner, but since he wasn't in the wedding, he didn't bother to go. No point torturing himself unnecessarily.

He refrained from a fist pump as another button slipped out.

"I've got two. At this rate, I'll have you out of this dress by suppertime tomorrow. I hope you're not in a rush to go anywhere."

"Well, our plane takes off tomorrow morning at nine o'clock to go to Rome. And we were touring Italy for our honeymoon as well as Switzerland."

"Wow. Sounds fun." He didn't really mean it, but he didn't know what else to say. It sounded fun for someone who wasn't him. Unless Ruby was with him.

"Don't lie. I know you would never want to do that."

He thought he heard her foot tapping on the floor.

"You love it on your farm, holed up here in the middle of nowhere, by yourself."

"Can't deny it."

"It wouldn't hurt you to get out a little bit."

"Probably wouldn't," he ground out, trying not to sound like he was growling his words but torn between frustration at how hard the buttons were to undo and even more frustration that he had to stand back there and stare at the sweet spot where her shoulder joined her neck and not kiss it like he wanted to.

"Well, good. I'm glad you agree. I've got a whole month's worth of travel and lodging already paid for. You and I might as well go and enjoy it."

Oh. He hadn't been expecting that.

How cruel life could be.

He was taking off her wedding dress and she'd just asked him to go with her on her honeymoon, but neither action meant what he wanted them to.

His fingers stilled before he forced them back into motion. Three buttons done.

From his calculations, he probably ought to do at least ten, so she wouldn't come back downstairs with her dress half off, begging him to do the rest.

Goodness help him, he was so tempted to ditch his responsibilities and fly off to some foreign country with the only woman he'd ever wanted.

Twisting the button, he forced himself to say the thing that needed to be said. "As exciting as a vacation in Rome or Switzerland or whatever you just said sounds, I'm going to have to decline."

"Why? Do you hate me that much?" She said it kind of like she didn't really think he hated her, but maybe she was just digging, or maybe she needed reassurance. After all, her fiancé of five years had just been with another woman. Maybe it was finally sinking in that it might mean he hadn't been happy with her.

"I don't hate you. Probably the opposite. But you already know that." He wasn't willing to say more. A man did have to have some pride, after all.

She looked over her shoulder, her eyes narrowed. "I already know what?"

"That I don't hate you." He jerked her button. "Stop moving. The stupid buttons are hard enough to undo. When you wiggle around underneath them, I lose it every time."

She stilled but didn't lose the bone she'd been chewing. "You said the 'opposite.' What did you mean by that?"

"I just kind of figured you'd just caught your fiancé with another woman, maybe you need to be assured that there are people who care about you. I'm one of those people."

Maybe he wouldn't have noticed it if his hands hadn't been on her back, but her backbone seemed to wilt, and some of the starch went out of her.

"Wesley and I kind of scoffed at the idea of love and all of those tingly feelings. We had a relationship built on mutual respect and friendship, and I had thought that would be enough. It was exactly what I wanted, since in my experience, watching my friends get married and subsequently get divorced, those tingly feelings fade, and then you claim to fall out of love."

She leaned her head back and looked at the ceiling. The button he was struggling with slipped out of his hand. He was pretty sure if this was their actual wedding night, he wouldn't have been patient enough to get the stupid thing off. Maybe one of the selling points was that it doubled as a nightgown.

She continued, blissfully unaware of his thoughts. "If you base your relationship on something else, you don't have to worry about that. That was the theory anyway. The theory that Wesley blew to pieces earlier today. But I can't say that my heart is broken. Because it's not. It wasn't involved at all." She snorted. "I will say my pride's hurt, and yeah, there's a little bit of thinking I guess I wasn't good enough. Why couldn't he have waited until we'd been married for twenty years before he decided I wasn't good enough? I might not care at that point."

He was a creep to do it now, and he'd have been a creep to do it in twenty years.

"Wouldn't it be much harder to walk away from twenty years of life together than it would be to walk away from five?" he murmured.

She wasn't being exactly logical right now. Although, he had to admit it certainly helped the green monster that had been sitting on his shoulder for the last five years to lie down and go to sleep when he heard she didn't really love Wesley.

It didn't help to hear that she didn't believe in love, though, because that didn't bode well for his future. Even if she did develop feelings for him, she'd probably deny them or walk away from them, because he wasn't what she wanted either.

Funny, how he'd convinced himself he could be okay with that. The wanting had never gone away; it had just gotten shifted to the side.

"So you're not interested in going on my honeymoon with me?

Not asking you to marry me. I'm just asking you to be my plus one. All the reservations are made for two."

"How do you know that Wesley isn't taking the florist's assistant and planning on doing the exact same thing with her?" He didn't mean it as a serious question, necessarily, but after he said it, he figured it was probably just as likely.

"Because she wasn't old enough to be out of high school."

"The older you get, the younger kids look."

She flicked her head around, her eyes narrowed. "Whose side are you on, anyway?"

Right. So he grinned.

If eyes could shoot sparks, he'd be on fire. It might be worth it, because she was gorgeous when she was angry.

"I am not. I'm scary and fearsome and a force to be reckoned with when I'm angry."

He hadn't meant to say that out loud, hadn't realized he had. It made his smile dim, which made her superior look grow even more so, and it was her turn to smile.

"At least you're acting more like the Ruby I know than the Ruby I've been with all afternoon."

"You've said that line before. Multiple times." Her voice was softer and thoughtful. "Every time, pretty much, you came to rescue me from myself when I wasn't sure I could keep doing what I needed to do in order to get to where I wanted to be."

He nodded. Anytime she'd called Race, and he'd talked to Ethan about the trials of becoming a doctor and how Ruby was struggling, Ethan had never been able to stop himself from going. At first, it was with Race's blessing. But eventually, he'd never even said anything to Race about it; he just went.

"You know, I owe you for all those times. You should come with me to Italy and Switzerland, just because you're part of the reason that I'm a surgeon today."

For the first time in his life, Ethan almost wished he could. He'd never been interested in going anywhere else, always loved the beauty of the Ozark foothills and his Arkansas home. Especially now that he had his own farm, he'd be quite content never setting foot off it.

But he could spend a month with Ruby.

Of course, he wouldn't be worth anything when she dropped him back off on his farm and walked away, out of his life and back to hers.

"I almost wish I could. But I can't."

"That's just an excuse, isn't it? You don't want to leave your farm." She turned around. "I'm sorry. I would feel the same way about my practice if I hadn't already scheduled this."

"No. That's not it, not really. I already have something scheduled for the next month."

"Something?"

"Nothing you'd be interested in." Not sure why he didn't want to tell her, he closed his mouth. Maybe he didn't want her to know because she'd see right through him.

"Try me. I've got the next month free."

He studied her buttons, realizing he couldn't not tell her without making a big deal of it. "I run a camp here for four weeks in June. I've done it every year since I bought the place. Just some boys, maybe ten, that are like me growing up, don't have much of anything, including family. I spend a month with them and just try to give them an idea that maybe there are some ways that they could go in their life to turn it around and maybe they don't have to be like their parents or let their environment define them."

Chapter Five

$\mathcal{E}$than had a camp?

It shouldn't surprise her, because he'd always tried to be helpful, looking for ways to do things for people in his own quiet way. He'd done so for her, of course, and her siblings, their parents.

He'd just always been there. Stalwart and faithful, quiet, ready to drift back into the shadows once he wasn't needed anymore.

She supposed that's why she'd assumed that he was spending his extra time on the farm now. Now that he had a place of his own.

The camp surprised her, but again, it shouldn't have.

At least it got her mind off his fingers on her back. His breath on her neck. His voice in her ear.

This wasn't the way she'd expected her dress to come off, but she almost wished it was for real.

The shivers that she had to control, the rippling tingles that went down her spine, and the way her heart flipped and flopped in her chest, they weren't unexpected either.

They weren't, but somehow, they still managed to surprise her.

"All boys?" She hadn't expected Ethan to be sexist.

His fingers stilled, and she felt herself straining to feel them move again.

Finally, when he didn't move and didn't say anything, she looked over her shoulder.

His chin lowered, and his eyebrows lifted.

"You know better," he said softly.

She narrowed her eyes, running back through her mind, trying to figure out why her first assumption—that he was sexist—was incorrect.

"It's just you?" she finally asked.

"Natalie and Mom come and cook lunch and clean up some for us. It's up to us to do breakfast and supper. A couple boys who used to be in the camp and are now teens come help."

There he was talking about Natalie again. Whoever she was.

Every time he said her name, it caused her shoulders to tighten and her stomach to feel sick.

She would never in a million years have said that she could be jealous of someone who rented a shack on the edge of somebody's farm, but hearing her name, the way it curled off Ethan's lips with almost a special kind of warmth to it, definitely triggered the yucky feelings in her stomach.

It had to be jealousy.

She'd long ago learned, just because she had "Dr." in front of her name now, it didn't make her any different than anybody else. It might make the way people looked at her different, it might make people think that she could do things she couldn't actually do, and it might give her a little more respect, but it hadn't changed *her*.

She was still human. Still prone to failure, still susceptible to human thoughts and emotions. As much as she wanted to think that she thought logically and not emotionally.

So yeah, he didn't have to tell her anything more about Natalie for her to know that she was definitely feeling jealousy.

Didn't mean she had to accept jealousy; she would fight it

because that was an emotion she didn't want to feel and not one that was acceptable either.

If he had a special place in his heart for Natalie, that was only good for her, because a man like Ethan would be a real catch for any woman. Natalie was one lucky lady.

"I'm not doing anything for the next month; you could have a girls' camp too."

His fingers had started working again, but they stopped, and his breath huffed out, skimming along her neck, tickling the hair, and making her close her eyes.

The seconds ticked by, with the man behind her frozen, but she knew he wasn't being dramatic. He just didn't say much, and he was probably thinking about what she said.

Sure enough, after about twenty seconds, he spoke. "You're sure about that?"

"You know I'm not the kind of person that starts something and doesn't finish it." To say the least.

"Yeah, but today's kinda fresh in your mind. Maybe next week this time, you're gonna wish that you'd chosen to do something else with your extra time."

"Well, I would kind of like to go on my honeymoon, but that's pretty much out of the question, since I haven't been able to convince anyone around here to go with me, so I might as well do the next best thing."

"And the next best thing is running a girls' camp for underprivileged girls?"

"Sure. I'm guessing it's probably not the most relaxing thing in the world, but it feels like something that would be good and necessary and helpful, and I love the idea. You've already got the perfect setup, and it'll take my mind off the crap that happened today and make me feel good about myself again. Why not?"

"I usually take the boys around the farm and teach them things like working with the animals, fixing fence, cutting wood. I actually have had loggers here on the property." That reminded him that Joe had texted and said he wouldn't be bringing a check around for a week or two. Something about his son cutting himself with a chainsaw on a different job and being in the hospital in Saint Louis. Ethan hoped it wasn't too bad. But the loggers were finished up and he'd love to be paid.

He shook his head. Where was he? "The boys and I will be working on cleaning up any branches and brush they've left behind. We do a lot of hands-on stuff outside. I'm guessing that you're probably not going to be teaching the girls to milk goats or pick berries."

He had a point. She didn't know anything about doing anything outside. She'd spent the last twelve years learning how to fix the inside of a person, and that didn't include going outside and chopping wood.

"So this is like a sexist, traditional camp where the girls have to sit inside and sew buttons?"

She supposed buttons were on the brain. She could have them redo her wedding dress. But that would be pointless work, since she never wanted to see the stupid thing again in her life.

"Not necessarily, although I guess I don't really appreciate the mocking in your tone, because there is a place for that. It's not like we have to take away one choice in order to present another. That's not really giving choices, is it?"

She pressed her lips closed. He was right. Just because she'd chosen a different path didn't mean that someone who wanted to choose something that was the opposite of what she had chosen wasn't correct. Maybe even better in some ways, because she'd deliberately chosen not to have children. What was the point in her having kids and giving them to someone else to raise?

Wesley and she had talked about that, and both of them could see the logic there.

It hadn't felt like a sacrifice at the time, but she was cognizant enough to know that as she lived her life, it might be a decision she regretted.

"I'm sorry. I didn't mean to sound like I was mocking anything. I guess I was just asking if I had to teach those things, or maybe I could do something else?"

"My thought has always been that I wanted them to learn something they probably weren't going to learn in their environment. Just to open up their worldview a little bit and show them that there might be a slightly different way that is just as good or better than the way that they'd be shown by the modeling of their parents or by what they learn in school."

Right. She could get that. She pulled her lips in and worried a little bit with her teeth while her fingers twisted the scissors.

"We can learn the things together. It can't be that hard."

"What things?" he asked, a slight tone of suspicion in his voice.

"I don't know. What 'traditional' things do girls do? Cook? We can figure that out. Lots of people do that, and it can't be hard. Sew? I don't even know if people do that anymore. But again, if I can pull someone's skin together and stitch it up, surely cloth can't be any more difficult. Gardening? I can do that. There's plenty of stuff on gardening on the web, I'm sure. I'll spend the weekend studying."

She'd spent plenty of weekends and late nights memorizing the ACLS manual. How hard could it be to thumb through a cookbook and learn that?

Then a thought occurred to her that startled her: maybe it was too late to find any girls who would come.

"I've been making an assumption that you can find girls. But if the camp starts in two days, maybe that's impossible."

"No. This has always been informal. The most I do is have the parents sign a couple of forms, and I'm sure all Dad would have to do is mention it from the pulpit on Sunday, and you'd have enough girls from there who want to come. I've turned boys away every year from just that much."

"Is that from where your boys come? From the congregation?"

"A couple are from Natalie, and a couple are from St. Louis, from a church that Dad knows there. There are a few from our congregation. We try to take the poorest of the poor."

Which led to another question for Ruby. "Who pays for this?"

There was a long pause. She felt a loosening in her back, as though another button popped open.

Eventually, he said, "I do."

He breathed out, and she felt the soft air over her exposed skin.

"I think you can get the rest of them."

She took a step and turned. "Can you afford to do a girls' camp?"

Even if he could, she had no idea if she could actually do this.

Of course, it wasn't common knowledge to most people, but about ninety-seven percent of the time in the OR, she had no idea or at least very little idea of whether she could or couldn't do what needed to be done. No two things were alike, especially in the OR.

No trauma was ever the same as another trauma, and no two people reacted the same to anything. There was always a set of unknowns, and solving the problems as she went along was part of the job.

Therefore, this was not unfamiliar territory to her, although it wasn't life and death, which actually made it a little relaxing, if she wanted to think about it like that.

Except, it was Ethan, and she had a feeling that whatever he did, he did it well. She wanted to be the same and be a help, not a hindrance.

"Yeah." No elaboration, just one word. He stepped back, leaning a hip against the counter as though he needed to put space between them, shoving his hands into his pockets. His eyes were hooded, his white shirt and black pants looking natural in a way she didn't expect.

She'd always been kind of partial to the rugged cowboy look, probably because of the way Ethan looked in high school, but he definitely looked good in his dress clothes.

"Can Natalie and your mom handle cooking for twice as many?" She hoped her curiosity about Natalie didn't come out in her words.

She wanted to know more. But she congratulated herself on her casual tone and figured he probably wouldn't know where she was going with it.

"The girls will be here; they can do the cooking. I usually make the boys cook breakfast for themselves, then we'll typically have something like hot dogs or mountain pies over the bonfire in the evening."

She wanted to accuse him of being sexist again, but she understood what he said he was doing. Teaching skills that the children might not learn anywhere else.

Except she had never really learned any of those skills.

Her sisters had. Penny had made sure of it.

Ruby had always been busy doing science experiments and dissecting stuff and... Her eyes widened.

Why not? Why couldn't she do the things she was good at with the girls? She twisted her tongue, biting down on it, which was something she always seemed to do when she was thinking intensely.

"You're thinking extra hard." Ethan crossed his arms over his chest, and his brows puckered.

She untwisted her tongue and set her jaw in what she hoped was a more relaxed looking position. "What in the world makes you think that?"

"That twisted tongue and clamping down expression you had. It's what you always do, in particular when you have an idea that you think is absolutely brilliant and you're looking at it from all different sides."

"How do you even know that about me?" He had hit it right on the head. What he'd said was totally accurate, but he shouldn't know her that well.

He lifted a shoulder and looked away.

His behavior struck her as odd. She didn't want to think about it, because she thought her idea was pretty fantastic.

"If you think you can get girls to come, I have a month, and I'd love to spend it here."

She realized it was absolutely true. Sure, she had the whole wedding thing looming over her head, and she needed to do something to handle it, and soon, but she was excited about doing something that benefited kids, and maybe she could save their lives *before* they hit the ER.

So much of what she saw in her job as a trauma surgeon was from people making poor decisions, but those decisions could be headed off years prior, if instead of thinking it was fun to hop in a car and go cruising in the middle of the night, kids had a purpose, and a plan, and things that they loved to do, and didn't feel like they needed to entertain themselves by doing crazy dangerous stuff.

The idea was intriguing. And something she'd never really thought about. In the years since her parents' death from being hit by a drunk driver, she had been focused on saving their lives by doing better surgery.

But what if their lives could have been saved if the person who hit them hadn't been drunk? What if that person, as a kid, had had someone like Ethan to guide him in a different direction for his life? What if he'd never started touching alcohol to begin with?

Those were new questions, and there were plenty of people around the world working on answers, but it was an angle she hadn't really considered for herself before. She liked it.

Ethan's eyes were hooded. He hadn't moved, studying her.

Maybe he was still concerned about whether or not she was actually going to stay. He didn't need to be. What else was she going to do? She didn't really want to face anyone, and she wasn't a huge social person anyway.

Sure, it would have been nice to tour Europe, see Italy, go to Switzerland... She'd never been. She spent her whole life working.

Honestly, she'd rather have a purpose than entertain herself. Especially now. That was just who she was. She loved the idea of having something meaningful to do for the next month rather than floating around.

She met his stare with one of her own—the determined look that she got when the steps of an operation solidified in her mind and she realized she really could save this person.

Maybe it was the look that convinced him, maybe it was something that he had thought in his head, whatever it was, his hands dropped, and he jerked his head down.

"You're gonna have to keep them entertained from the time they get up in the morning 'til they go to bed at night. They're here from Monday morning until Friday night. They go home Saturday and Sunday and are back again Monday. The last week, we have Christmas in July, where we kinda give them a Christmas like they might not get at their house. The week before that, we spend decorating for it. I've got a buddy who is a stuntman in Hollywood and has access to a fake snowmaker. He brings that for us."

Wow. He was more organized than she'd figured. Her fingers itched. She was excited, and yeah, the whole Christmas thing made everything even more special. She could totally get into this.

"I'm getting changed, then I need to make some phone calls about the wedding—" She looked around. "Oh my goodness. I don't have my phone. I think...I think I left it at the church."

"That would be the reason it's not ringing off the hook right now," Ethan said with a heavy dose of sarcasm in his voice. "Maybe that's the reason mine is."

"I hadn't noticed."

"I shut it off. You can use it after you're done changing. In the meantime, I'll take care of Mom and Dad. And I'll inform Mom and Natalie about doubling the food they were planning on making, and I'll see if Dad will give us names of any girls who might be interested, and we can gather a few up. How many do you think you can handle?"

"You said you're doing ten?"

"I didn't start out with ten."

"I think I can handle that." How hard could it be? "How old?"

"Mine are usually around eleven to fourteen. I might have a fifteen-year-old to help this year if he didn't get a job."

"You don't even know?"

"I told him he could come if he wanted to help. But he was trying to find a job, and if he's got one, I'm not expecting him."

She nodded. This was pretty much the weirdest thing she'd ever heard of. So loosey-goosey, and yet so good.

"Bedroom's first door on the right?" she asked as she walked out.

"That's right. Help yourself to anything."

She looked back at the odd note in his voice, but his face revealed nothing, and she figured she must have imagined it. She headed upstairs, trying not to wonder why Ethan had managed to impress her so much.

Chapter Six

Five hours later, Ethan looked out the back window at Ruby, her legs drawn up and tucked underneath her, the notebook she'd asked to borrow from him open in front of her with various pieces of paper scattered all around her, scribbling furiously with the pen she'd also borrowed, a highlighter lying nearby, its use obvious by the big, bright lines of green spotting all the papers.

She'd borrowed his phone and occasionally picked it up, typing the password that he'd given her easily and apparently looking things up on the internet. She tapped the pen to her head and twisted her tongue, biting down on it.

He'd probably given a little bit too much of himself away with that tongue comment. But he'd seen her do it so often, every time he visited her. Studying, running through in her mind whether she really wanted to put the work in to realizing her dream, and when he'd said something that she didn't agree with, but she couldn't articulate why.

He'd always loved watching her do it.

But yeah, it probably was weird that he knew it.

Still, he had to admire how she dove into things.

It had taken about an hour to deal with the wedding issues. His parents had already pretty much defused everything, and he supposed that Ruby would have some fallout to deal when it came to the physicians that had been invited and her friends.

But she'd put that out of her mind and threw herself into the camping project, and he knew that the girls his dad was able to scrounge up would be blessed because of it.

Ruby had said she could handle ten, but Ethan had asked his dad to try to limit it to five. One of Natalie's girls, Maggie, was old enough, and he'd ask his dad to include her. He was sure Natalie would want to send her.

Ethan opened the door and poked his head out.

Ruby glanced up, blinking like she was coming out of a trance.

"You hungry?" He figured it was a toss-up, depending on how upset she was about the wedding.

Her brows pushed down, as though she had to think about it, before her face brightened.

"I am." She sounded surprised, and he had to bite back a laugh. "Do you need me to help you make something?" She glanced at the stuff strewn all over the table and started gathering it up.

"No. I already made spaghetti. I have a bit of a salad to go with it. I can bring it out if you want."

Her eyes widened again, like she hadn't even considered eating outside.

He never ate in if he could eat out.

"Sure. Actually, I'll help you." She grabbed the rest of her stuff and stepped out of the picnic table seat, carrying it all in. "Thank you so much for letting me use your phone. Do you think we could make a trip to town?"

She handed his phone back as she went through the doorway.

He took it from her, careful not to touch her. Just instinct. After all, undoing the buttons on her dress was enough temptation for one day.

"We can. If you don't mind waiting until tomorrow, we can do it after church. That way we only have to make one trip into town, but if you can't wait, I don't have anything pressing to do tonight."

"Aren't you getting ready? You have ten boys descending on you next week, for four weeks, isn't there anything you need to do?"

Her voice sounded incredulous, but she was walking away from him, and he couldn't see her face.

"I'm not going to do anything special with them. I'm just gonna do what we always do. I mean, I did get enough axes and knives and matches to make sure that all the boys have some, but we'll make what we need as we need it. I am not going to do it for them. That's part of why they're coming."

He supposed he should have stopped talking as soon as he said axes and knives, because she had whirled around on him.

"Do you realize how many kids end up in the ER because of accidents that could be avoided?"

It was like she thought he didn't know the danger. "So we shouldn't do anything because we might get hurt? You want us to sit around at the kitchen table and stare at each other? Maybe we could knit. But, wait, knitting needles are pointed. Maybe we shouldn't do that either?"

"Sarcasm doesn't become you, Ethan. You're the strong, silent type, remember?" She gave him that look, and her tone said she was the oldest and used to putting her brothers down. To defending her position over his egregious breach of what was socially acceptable.

But he wasn't one of her brothers, and *he* was the oldest.

"I was just trying to figure out what you want me to do."

"It's possible to have fun without hurting yourself."

"It's possible to eat without enjoying it. Why would you want to?"

Her eyes narrowed just a little bit as she rounded the table as though thinking about what he said.

"So we should just eat candy bars and drink chocolate milk every day?"

"It isn't that. But things sometimes make us miserable, and I wonder why in the world you'd want to live if you're that miserable all the time. I think the same thing probably applies to doing dangerous things. What's the point of living if you don't have fun?"

"And I think we're back to where we were before, you can have fun without doing something dangerous."

"You can't tell me you live that way. I've seen you. You don't think it's not dangerous to drive home after a thirty-six-hour shift?"

"That was necessary. I didn't do that for fun."

"You enjoyed every minute of it." Maybe his tone was accusatory, but it was true.

Her lips tightened, because she knew she couldn't argue. Her eyes swept the table, and her mouth opened. "That's interesting. That looks like a salad. From the man who was just complaining about what the point of eating was if he didn't enjoy it."

"That's spinach and lettuce from my garden, and bacon from the hog I butchered this winter."

"I suppose you made the cheese too?"

He snorted. "Sarcasm doesn't become you either, Dr. Barclay."

Her mouth opened, and her eyes shot to his. She didn't say anything for a good three seconds. He wondered what he'd done.

"I think that's the first time you've used my title."

"I'm sorry. I didn't realize you preferred it. I can call you Dr. Barclay from now on."

"Don't be ridiculous. It sounds ridiculously stupid coming from you."

"And how am I different than anyone else?" His heart skipped a beat or six because he wanted to be different than everyone else to her. But that wasn't really what he meant, and she didn't take it like that anyway.

"I've never really thought of you as my brother, but you're definitely one of the people that have always been there for me in my life. Don't you even start calling me Dr. Barclay."

"Even for camp? The kids are going to have to call you something. What do you want?" He hadn't had time to consider what they should call her. The boys just mostly called him Mr. Ethan. He was fine with it if a few of them didn't put the mister in front. He tried to gently correct them, not because he felt it was necessary for his ego or pride, but because he thought it was good for them to learn a little respect for adults.

"Miss Ruby is fine," she said, a little slowly as though testing the title out on her lips.

"Dr. Ruby?"

He'd make the kids call her that if she wanted. She'd earned that title. He'd seen the work and sweat and blood and tears she'd put in, the days she'd wanted to quit, and the days he'd wanted her to quit, when he could hardly stand to see how rundown and exhausted she was.

But she persevered through it all, even the months of cadaver dissection, which would have sent him running screaming out of the door, leaving any dreams of becoming a doctor behind, but she'd done it gamely and even joked about it some toward the end, although he'd always heard her speaking respectfully of the person who'd donated their body for her education.

An invaluable resource and something he'd never even considered doing.

So much in life one didn't know until one was with someone whose realm extended out of one's own, comfortable zone.

"No. I don't think so. I earned the title, and I love it, but I think I'd like to leave that part of me behind for a little bit."

He wished he hadn't said anything, because she sounded sad. It was the first time that she sounded contemplative or even a little bit upset. It did gratify him to know that what Wesley had done hadn't really hurt her. At least not that she showed. Maybe she would cry into her pillow tonight, but he doubted it.

They carried the food out to the picnic table. He usually didn't.

Typically, he just went out and sat down on the steps with Slipper and Crimson beside him.

Sometimes he just ate right out of the pan. But he figured he'd better be a little bit more civilized with company here. With Ruby here.

There might not ever be a chance for him to be with Ruby, which was his dream, but he didn't have to act like a caveman around her either.

After they were done eating, she helped with the dishes. He was looking forward to sitting outside with her. The most beautiful time of the day was as the sun went down and evening fell around.

But after she cleaned out the pan, she said, "If you don't mind, I think I'm going to go upstairs. I'm exhausted. And if I'm going to get up and go to church tomorrow, I'm going to have to face a lot of people that I would rather not. At least not right now. I think I'd like to turn in early."

He'd not considered that. Tomorrow would be a hard day for her. Time would make it easier.

"We don't have to go if you don't want to. There's no need."

"I need to go to town to get supplies. You said we'd do that after church."

"We can do it instead of church. I understand why you might not want to go to town. I certainly won't make you."

"I'm not going to be a coward."

"It's not being a coward to give yourself a little bit of time to heal, to let a little bit of water pass under the bridge."

She closed her mouth and looked away. She knew about healing. And how it took time. What he said obviously made sense to her.

"I appreciate that. Thank you."

She turned and walked out of the kitchen, and he waited for her to leave before he put his hands on the counter and braced himself, dropping his head down. He was gonna spend more time with Ruby in the next four weeks than he ever had in his life before, and he was pretty sure he was going to fall deeper in love with her every single day.

And then she was going to walk out and go back to her surgeon's life.

He just hoped he could handle it.

Chapter Seven

*S*unday evening, Ethan sat on his front porch step, his back leaning against the banister, one leg stretched out in front of him with his arm resting on it, his other leg planted two steps down.

It was always nice to have someone to share the beauty with.

Not even someone to talk to, although he'd listen, happily, as long as they didn't expect him to say anything too profound, because he could look at and enjoy but often not be able to say what moved him so deeply about this time of day.

Regardless, having someone to talk to hadn't ever been a problem.

Ruby was in his house now. They'd gotten back from their shopping trip, and he'd taken her on a tour of the farm on his ATV, showing her the boundary lines.

It had taken several hours, and he'd recommended she take a shower when they were done, just because they'd gone through some brush and trees and he didn't want to see her get bitten by a tick.

He was going in in a bit and taking a shower, too, but for now, he was enjoying the evening.

The rumble of a car on gravel came over the evening air, and he listened for a while before the car actually came into sight.

It was a pickup, and he recognized it immediately as Denver's, Ruby's brother's truck.

Denver parked beside the house, considerate enough to not block the view. The door slammed, and his tall, slender younger brother came walking around the side of the house.

A far cry from the gangly boy he'd been the first time Ethan had seen him, Denver had filled out and walked with confidence.

Ethan enjoyed talking to him. Denver had a strength of character that wasn't often found in a man and a steady confidence that almost screamed he could do anything he put his mind to.

As an underwater welder, he probably needed that kind of confidence. The job was downright dangerous, and it kept him away from home.

"Hey, man," Denver said as he came up the steps and held his hand out.

Ethan shook it without getting up and jerked his head. "Good to see you. Have a seat."

Denver settled on the top step, his feet planted on the third step and his elbows resting on his knees.

He looked out over the view that Ethan had been enjoying, his eyes taking it all in, and his body relaxed, like he liked what he saw.

"Wouldn't be hard to settle down to this," he finally said.

"It's gorgeous, that's for sure." Ethan didn't have a hard time imagining Denver settling down. He did, however, have a hard time trying to picture a woman who was good enough for his brother.

"I thought Ruby was here," Denver said, almost studiously casual.

"She is. Last I heard, she was going to take a shower. We've got a bunch of kids coming to camp tomorrow. Maybe she's feeling a little overwhelmed."

"Missed you guys in church today."

"I miss you most of the time." Denver was hardly ever home. In fact, before Ruby's wedding, Ethan thought it was Christmas since he'd been home last.

"It's been six months since I've been there. I expected to see my brother and my sister. Kind of surprised I didn't."

"I think you can understand it was probably pretty hard for Ruby to face all of that. I told her to give it some time, and that'll make it easier. I think part of her was torn, and she did want to go. Seeing you was a fairly big draw. I'm glad you stopped in."

"I dropped some bags off on the back porch. Mom made sure to get Ruby's clothes and her cell phone, her purse, and a few other things. I think she thought she'd give them to you guys in church, but I became the delivery boy when you didn't show up." He flashed a white smile in Ethan's direction.

"Mom's smart sometimes. I bet she knew Ruby wanted to see you."

"Yeah. I'm heading back to the oil wells tomorrow, wanted to see her before I go."

Denver didn't say, but Ethan figured he was thinking his job was dangerous, and he never knew if it would be the last time he'd see his family.

"Why don't you quit? Your job pays gold bricks. You can't be working for money anymore. Come back up. Settle down. This view isn't exclusive to my house and farm. There are plenty of other places that are almost as nice." Ethan knew he was a little partial to Sweet Rest Farm, but he was saying the truth. There were plenty of places for Denver to settle down.

"Yeah or no. I guess I admire you for doing it by yourself. I can, I know it. But it just almost feels like defeat if I quit and come back, for no reason other than..." He held his hands up. "Why? What's the point?"

Ethan didn't say anything. He figured Denver was probably thinking about a wife, but there was also his purpose in life.

Ethan struggled with that some too.

"Is it better than what you're doing? You want something more meaningful?"

"I'm doing work that needs to be done. I'm making things safer for a bunch of men who have families they're working to support. I can justify that in my head." He shrugged. "Coming back and retiring, so to speak, living for myself, because this is what I would love to do, where's the higher purpose in that? I just don't see it."

Maybe that was part of what this time of day brought out, the contemplative thoughts, the questioning, or maybe that was just being an older brother and someone who didn't talk much. When he didn't say anything, people had a tendency to fill that silence with their own words, and all he had to do was listen. That's all most people wanted anyway.

The sun had gone down, and the air had started to get cooler, when they heard a car motor and stones crackling under tires.

"Someone is coming," Denver said, cocking his head.

Ethan nodded. He thought for a minute then said, "I bet it's Natalie. She's probably bringing the groceries and stuff for tomorrow so she doesn't have to unload her car at her house and then load it back up tomorrow morning."

She'd probably done her shopping tonight.

"Natalie? Girlfriend?" Denver hitched an eyebrow, and half of his mouth curled up.

Ethan shook his head. No smile on his face. "Natalie is my neighbor. She's had it pretty rough since she took her kids and left her alcoholic husband. I think he was slapping her around, and one night he did a little more than that." Natalie had never really said, other than she'd come from just north of Austin and figured she was far enough here to be away from him.

Ethan had simply told her that if her husband ever showed up, she could call him and he'd be there. Not because of any love affair on his part, but just because that was the decent thing to do, because the idea of some man physically harming his wife made Ethan's blood steam.

"Slimeball," Denver muttered.

"Yeah, she's had a time of it. He doesn't pay any support, of course, and she has five kids. All little."

"I see." Denver nodded like he truly did.

She wasn't a charity case, just a neighbor helping a neighbor. For Natalie, he'd do pretty much anything. Again, not because of any special attraction or love affair on his part. Just because it was a decent thing to do.

"She cooks for you?" Denver asked, his eyes hooked on the SUV that had come over the rise and started down the tree-lined drive.

"She helps Mom with lunch for the camp."

Denver jerked his head.

A few minutes later, Natalie pulled in around the side to the door closest to the kitchen.

"Come on, you can help me carry the stuff in."

Ethan stood, and Denver straightened up beside him. They walked around and reached Natalie's car as she got out.

She leaned back into her car. "You guys sit tight. We'll be here tomorrow, and you can get out then, but it's late tonight, and we're going to go back home and get to bed." She gave the kids in the car a last look before she stepped away and slammed her door shut.

"Hey, Ethan," she said cheerfully. "I've got the stuff in the back. I figured it'd be okay if I bring it in tonight. I'm sorry I didn't call." She pushed some flyaway hair back away from her face. "It's a bit of a hassle shopping with five kids. Never easy." She rolled her eyes a little and sounded less frazzled than he thought she should, considering that it couldn't be the slightest bit easy shopping with five small children.

"This is Denver." Natalie had probably seen him maybe once or twice in church, but since she'd just moved into the area and Denver wasn't around much, he figured he'd introduce them.

"Nice to meet you, Denver. I don't recall seeing you around."

Denver, who was never rude to anyone, said, "That's because I haven't been."

Ethan's gaze ripped to Denver, who had sounded annoyed, but maybe he was thinking more about Natalie's husband and didn't realize how his words were coming out.

"This is Natalie," Ethan said, not because Denver didn't know, but because Denver wasn't saying anything else.

Denver started walking to the back of the SUV.

Natalie's eyebrows bounced, but she followed him. "I think if we each take a big load, we can get them all in one trip."

Ethan had to agree, and they took as much as they could carry, with Natalie bringing up the rear.

When Ethan walked in, Ruby was coming down the stairs, and Ethan just about swallowed his tongue.

Her eyes got big, like she hadn't realized they had visitors, which made sense if she was in the shower when they came. He saw the slight hesitation in her descent, and he understood it. She looked like she had shorts on, and hopefully, that's what Denver and Natalie assumed.

But Ethan recognized his boxers. And she had another one of his T-shirts on, but instead of letting this one hang down to mid-thigh, she'd tied it in a knot, and a little bit of her stomach peeked out as she moved gracefully down the steps in her bare feet, all long, slender legs and big smiles as soon as she recognized Denver.

"Denver! I didn't realize you were here," she said, speeding up and striding to Denver, putting her arms around his neck.

Denver hugged her back. "I brought a bunch of your clothes that were packed in Wesley's car. Good thing, too, apparently, since you can now stop walking around the house in Ethan's underwear."

Yeah. It would've been too much for Denver not to notice that.

Natalie made a small choking noise, and Ethan tried to pull his eyes away from Ruby, although it felt like an almost superhuman effort, and in the back of his mind, he wondered how in the world he was going to be able to do camp with ten boys when all he wanted to do was stand and stare at the woman who made his clothes look far better than he ever could.

"Natalie, this is Ruby." He couldn't bring himself to say "my sister." He just couldn't. "Ruby, this is Natalie, my neighbor."

"So nice to meet you, Ruby," Natalie said, her hand out.

Something crossed Ruby's features, something weird, an expression that Ethan had never seen before. But it was gone in an instant. Ruby dropped her arms from around Denver's neck and shook Natalie's proffered hand.

"Just in the short time I've been here, Ethan has talked so much about you. He obviously thinks very highly of you. He said you're helping with camp tomorrow?"

"I am. One of my boys, Jack, will be here, and in church, they said that girls were welcome, so I signed Maggie up. She's over the moon. Normally she helps me cook, so she's really excited thinking she's going to be using an ax and chopping down trees in the woods." Natalie slanted laughing eyes at Ethan. "I haven't disabused her of that notion at this point," Natalie said, with an undercurrent of humor in her voice, as she looked at Ruby, who looked more like a model off a runway in New York City than she did like someone who would be tramping around in the woods brandishing an ax and chopping anything down.

"Well, I don't think we're going to quite be doing that, but I think she's going to have a lot of fun. I've had a lot of ideas, and I can't wait to share them with the kids," Ruby said.

Ethan had no trouble believing it. He wanted to chime in and tell Natalie how hard Ruby had worked on this. He also kind of wanted to brag about her being a surgeon, but he did neither. If Ruby wanted people to know, she could tell them. He'd just concentrate on trying to look anywhere but her legs and the bit of midriff and anywhere else on Ruby since even her elbow looked sexy to him.

He fastened his eyes on the ceiling. That seemed like a good place to look while longing with all his heart to go out and look at the sunset. He could look at that without getting into any trouble.

"Well, I'd like to stay and chat about it, but I left all my kids in the car. They're usually well behaved, but they're still kids, and one of them might get the bright idea of deciding that they need to take my car for a spin while I'm not in it, and that could be a problem, so I'm going to head out." Natalie made a noise with her mouth, which seemed to indicate she might not quite be fast enough to keep up with all her kids all the time, and she waved a hand as she left.

"She seems like a really nice girl," Ruby said thoughtfully, almost as though she'd expected to meet Natalie and not like her for some reason.

Ethan could have told her she would love Natalie, but her use of the word "girl" surprised him.

"You think she's that young?" he asked, wondering why he'd never seen that until Ruby said something.

Ruby grunted. "If she's even twenty-three, I'd be shocked."

"But she has five kids."

"So?" Ruby looked at him and tilted her head like she was going to need to explain basic biology to him.

He held a hand up. Never mind.

"Good to see you, Ruby," Denver said. Ethan had almost forgotten his brother was there. He hadn't said anything, hadn't moved since Natalie walked out. "I'm going to head out, too."

"You're not staying?" Ethan asked. Sometimes Denver had given him a hand with camp for a day or two.

"No. I have to be back in the gulf early tomorrow morning. I left your stuff on the porch. Take care, sis." Denver wrapped Ruby in his arms once more but then left almost like the house was on fire, and his pickup followed Natalie's SUV out the lane.

"That was weird. I thought he'd come to see you."

"He brought my clothes." Ruby moved an arm down, indicating her outfit. "You only had one pair of jeans left. I didn't want to wear them and you not have anything for tomorrow. I was going to wash clothes, if that's okay."

"There are more jeans up there. They're just in the closet."

"I'm sorry. I looked, but I guess I didn't look deep enough."

"It's perfectly okay to do laundry though. I'm not gonna turn that down." He grinned a little.

"I didn't figure you would. I certainly wouldn't either. But I do seem to recall you doing my laundry once or twice for me so I could study, and I figure I owe you at least two loads."

"Seriously? We're keeping track like that?"

"Well, I wasn't, when it was me owing you, but as soon as I catch up, yep, we're keeping track. Because I'm not going to do your laundry for the rest of my life."

Ethan nodded. He thought she was probably being funny, but her words were accurate—she wasn't going to be some man's wife, not in a traditional sense.

He didn't want anything else, although he wanted Ruby.

Still, on the farm, things would need to be a little more traditional. Not that he was afraid to do his own laundry, and not that he minded doing hers, because he wasn't and he didn't.

"I guess I'll go take a shower. I'll probably go to bed. Tomorrow is going to be a big day." He was back to staring at the ceiling again.

"Yeah. I'm ready for bed too."

"I'll walk out and grab your stuff and carry it in."

"Thanks."

"Have you talked to Wesley at all?" He didn't mean to ask that, but it felt weird that she was supposed to marry the man yesterday and had gone a whole day without talking to him after everything went down.

"I guess we'll see if he called my phone. But no, I haven't called him. And no one that I've talked with has said that he's been desperate to reach me, although maybe they've shut him down because they assume that I probably don't want to talk to him. That would be a correct assumption."

They walked out, and she grabbed her purse, along with a smaller over-the-shoulder bag, which Ethan assumed probably held her laptop and chargers, while he grabbed two large suitcases.

He followed her inside. She fished through her purse and pulled out her cell phone.

After clicking on it for a few seconds, she said, "He's called twenty-one times. The last time was thirty-seven minutes ago." She dropped her hand and turned to him. "Is it wrong of me to not talk to him?"

That was a tough question. Ethan didn't want to give a superficial answer, even though he wanted to shout, "No!"

He blew out a breath, studying the ceiling. "I think you definitely ought to forgive him. But from the way you're acting, that doesn't seem like it's going to be something that's hard for you. As for talking to him...no. I don't think it's wrong of you to not talk to him. I can't even believe that someone would do what he did and think that he could just call you up."

"Maybe I'll listen to his messages and make sure he didn't need anything important." She paused. "Probably all he wanted was to tell me that he was going to be taking that girl on our honeymoon, so I didn't think I would still be going."

He snorted. "That could be it."

She walked up the stairs in front of him, and he kept his eyes on the banister, admiring the old woodwork that was shiny and worn and of a quality that one didn't typically see in modern-day houses. Anything to keep his eyes and mind off the legs in front of him.

He didn't usually have a problem with legs.

Of course, they weren't usually covered with his boxers either.

They got to the top of the stairs, and she stood back as he set the suitcases in her room.

He walked back out without looking at anything. He didn't want to have that picture in his mind.

Not a room, not a bed, not legs. He didn't want any of it. He'd always been a big believer in if it wasn't yours, you shouldn't want it.

That applied doubly to a woman.

When two people got married, they belonged to each other.

Ruby wasn't married. Somehow God had worked that out. But she still didn't, and most likely never would, belong to him.

So he averted his eyes and walked back out.

But he couldn't stop from saying, "If you need anything, just let me know."

"I know," she said softly. "I know you'll take care of me."

He grinned, his hand on the doorknob to his room. "It is kinda cool to have a doctor on staff."

She snorted. "I don't know how much help I'll be with only my emergency bag. I'm not going to be doing open-heart surgery."

He hadn't wanted to, but he turned. She held up the bag he'd assumed was a laptop. "Emergency bag?"

"Never leave home without it."

"Got any good drugs in there?" He winked.

"Nothing I'm sharing with you." She smirked at him.

"If I remember correctly, you sleep pretty soundly. Maybe I'll do some snooping tonight."

"You don't remember correctly. I'm a featherlight sleeper, and I will wake as soon as you set foot out of your bed."

He laughed outright at that. "You told me, maybe a year or two ago, that during residency, you learned to lie down and fall asleep immediately, because you never knew when your next five minutes of sleep would come. I doubt you've outgrown that."

"Busted."

"Hand the drugs over now. No one gets hurt."

She laughed. "Nope. Not even a Tylenol." Her chin jerked. "Which, by the way, you ought to avoid taking."

"I'll keep that in mind. I do have a stock of Tylenol, and I'll probably use them this week for the minor aches and pains that I'm sure to end up with, since I'm getting older, and it's a little harder to keep up with all the young whippersnappers."

"You're not getting older, Ethan."

He shook his head. "Each year, life goes by faster. It's kind of shocking, but I can't believe I'm in my thirties. I know I'm going to blink, and when I open my eyes, I'll be sixty, and I'll wonder where my life went."

"Don't talk like that. It's depressing."

"But true. I want to get to that point, look back, and see a life well lived. I want to wring everything I can from it and do everything I can to be a blessing to others. Because I think living it for myself, I'll look back and find it was a waste."

She nodded, and he felt like she understood. "That's why I wanted to be a surgeon. I mean, it started out with my parents, but you can't imagine how good it feels to make a difference in somebody's life, *with* someone's life, or to have someone who might have—probably would have—died, but under your hands, they're saved. It's not like playing God exactly, but it's like working with God, a little. I can't even explain it." She shook her head, at a loss for words, and he could understand why.

He could almost feel what she was talking about, and for the first time, he was a little jealous. "That would be pretty amazing. Working hand in hand with the Lord."

"Maybe it's fanciful thinking, but there's just times I feel like that's the way it is. I can't even begin to explain the feeling, but I know it's what I was born to do." She looked around, realizing she was maybe getting a little personal.

Not that he minded. Not at all. He would never turn down getting to know more about Ruby and digging into what made her tick. She fascinated him in a way he couldn't explain. In a way that no one else did.

"Although..." She gave him a little grin. "I kinda feel like maybe doing this camp might keep people from even being in the ER to begin with. Like, showing them a different way will prevent them from doing some of the stupid things I see people doing that make them wind up on the operating table in front of me. Or the stupid things someone else was doing that made the innocent person in front of me wind up there."

He nodded, totally getting what she was saying. "That's exactly right. Giving them the idea that there might be a different choice. That maybe there's a different way of life than the one they come from. Even if you just show them that there's a different way to live."

"I like that too. Definitely, it's another thing that feels like you're working in tandem with the Lord, and there's nothing that could be more satisfying."

In that, at least, they were in agreement.

Chapter Eight

Things got a little crazy on Monday morning as the kids came in.

They started out in a trickle when Natalie came with her children, her son Jack carrying his duffel and his sleeping bag to the barn and her daughter Maggie coming into the house with her.

"Ethan said the girls are going to be sleeping in the living room?"

"That's right," Ruby said, her voice ringing with authority, even though she hadn't had a clue up until that second where the girls were going to sleep. She'd been so concerned about what in the world she was going to do with them all day she hadn't even considered what was going to happen at night.

"I thought you were just making lunch?" she asked as Natalie bustled around the kitchen.

"I've thrown some things in the crockpots for lunch, and I figured I'd make some waffles for the kids who came without eating. When Pastor Race comes, he'll be bringing kids that have been up since five or six o'clock, and they might not have eaten before they left."

Ruby nodded, helping Maggie with her stuff and finding her easy to talk to, despite their very different lives.

It had been a while since she had chatted with children other than during appointments. Typically, when she worked on her patients, they were already out, and she didn't have to try to make small talk.

But she didn't have to worry about talking to one girl for long, because it wasn't long until Race pulled in, and things got really nuts.

"You're looking a little overwhelmed," Ethan said as he walked in and saw her standing in the middle of the hall, trying to remember all the girls' names.

He had a fifty-pound sack of potatoes over his shoulder, and she assumed he was headed toward the kitchen.

"No more overwhelmed than I felt in the OR the time I accidentally severed an artery. Blood squirted everywhere, and my tech fainted dead away."

"Probably not the best place for him to be if he can't stand the sight of blood."

"He was a she, and she was nine months pregnant. She was in labor and had not told anyone, thinking she could make it through the operation, and she had been having a contraction, holding her breath, and happened to take that moment to pass out." She shivered, remembering. "Things got a little dicey in there for a while. But no one died, and that usually makes it a good day in the OR." She grinned. "I think that'll make it a good day here, too. Agree?"

"We have slightly higher standards here than you do in the OR, apparently," Ethan said, shaking his head and hefting the potatoes up a little higher, before he turned and walked into the kitchen.

She listened as he and Natalie chatted, and she forced the back of her neck to loosen. Whatever Ethan and Natalie were together was none of her business.

It wasn't hard to take her mind off them as the girls gathered shyly around.

Ruby sat cross-legged on the living room floor, waiting for one more girl, when Penny peeked her head around the corner.

"Hey, Mom," Ruby said. "Come on in. I want to introduce the girls to you. Ethan said you'd probably take one or two every day and cook with them. Is that right?"

Her mom stepped in, always smiling. Maybe it was Ruby's imagination, but she seemed to be especially happy to see her. She hadn't spent too much time under Penny's roof, but they had spent a lot of time on the phone together. At first, because Penny called her, but eventually she was comfortable enough to call Penny for advice too.

"That's right. In fact, I was getting ready to make some biscuits from scratch and cut up some fruit for salad. Who's helping today?"

One of the older girls with bright yellow clips contrasting with the deep blackness of her hair jumped up with her hand in the air. "Me! Me! My aunt watches the baking channel all the time, and I want to be a chef when I grow up. Please, please let me help?"

Ruby wasn't entirely sure of her name...Jasmine? Yeah. She thought that was right.

"That's fine, Jasmine. I'm sure Miss Penny will be happy to have you." Her gaze went around the room, looking at each girl. "This is my mom. You can call her Miss Penny."

She felt like an idiot.

Should she be sitting on the floor? She should be leading them through a tour of the kitchen and helping them get familiar with the house and looking a lot more competent than what she'd shown.

What kind of camp leader was she?

But none of the kids seemed to notice, and they chorused together, "Hi, Miss Penny."

"She'll be cooking lunch for us every day. And she'll be helping us clean up. Everyone will get a chance to work with her, so if you wanted to work today and you didn't get a shot, there'll be plenty of other opportunities."

"Is this all of us there's going to be?" Maggie asked.

"Here's the last girl," Natalie said as she walked into the living room beside a thin girl that was almost as tall as Natalie. "This is

Ava, and she's originally from Dallas, but her mom's aunt lives in Little Rock. That's where Ava's staying right now."

Natalie grinned at Ruby and gave her a wink before she slipped back out.

Her mom had already left, holding onto Jasmine's hand, leaving Ruby sitting in the middle of the floor with four girls and hoping she hadn't bitten off more than she could chew.

She'd said she'd handled worse in the ER, but what she hadn't mentioned, and what had been going through her mind, was her patients were all unconscious and she'd never had to actually keep track of anyone, because no one, through all the surgeries that she'd done, had ever gotten up off the table.

She kinda thought this was going to be a little different.

"OKAY, boys, at least half of you have been here before, so you know the first thing we're going to do is scrub down the bathroom that's out here from top to bottom, and then we'll climb the hayloft and get all of our stuff settled up there."

Ethan looked around the group of boys, most of them familiar and grinning up at him. The boys had never complained about cleaning the bathroom, because they knew there were plenty of other things they'd be doing that they'd enjoy.

"After we get done with all of that, I'll hand out throwing knives and scabbards for everyone, and I'll give you a few lessons on learning to throw them. I think it's warm enough that we'll spend the afternoon at the river, swimming. And of course we'll have a campfire this evening." The boys were young enough he didn't think this next bit was going to be too tricky. "There are going to be some girls around this year too, so we'll have to share the river, and they'll be a part of our campfire. No weapons at the campfire. Any questions?"

If there was one thing that Ethan knew after doing the camp for so many years, it was that his best-laid plans seldom came to fruition.

He had intended to take it easy the first day, doing things that kept him around the house, like the knife throwing and the bathroom scrubbing and going to the river which was not very far—just a quarter of a mile down the hill from the house—where he could keep an eye on Ruby and make sure everything was going okay with her and give her a hand if she needed it.

It didn't work out that way.

The cows in the upper pasture ended up getting out where the loggers had dropped a tree branch on his fence. He took all ten boys with him to put them back in, saw the tree up and fix the fence.

They ended up being gone through lunch and most of the afternoon until they got the cows in and the fence repaired and fixed the places where the cows had redecorated the neighbor's yard.

It worked out, because the neighbor had cherry trees that were ripe, and he arranged for the boys to come the next afternoon and pick cherries. They would give some to the tree owners, keep some for themselves, and give some to Pastor Race to distribute among parishioners who could use them.

Ethan made a note to keep some back for Natalie too. Not to mention there'd be cherries to eat all week at camp as well.

Still, by the time they got back, the boys were ready to get a bonfire started with the wood they'd cut up earlier and eat supper.

Ruby and the girls were in the vegetable garden, and as Ethan went by, Ruby looked up, her hair in wild disarray around her face, her mouth pinched, holding her iPad like it was surgically attached. She looked completely overwhelmed.

Chapter Nine

Ruby held her iPad in one hand while trying to make the picture bigger with her fingers.

Ethan's garden was surrounded by a white picket fence, and all five girls were in the garden with her. She cautioned them not to step on anything, because, to be frank, she had no clue which green things poking out of the ground were weeds, and which ones were things that were supposed to be there.

"This is what a carrot plant looks like, girls." She held the screen up so that all the girls could see. It didn't have big leaves but just kind of feathery, lacy-looking leaves. And in the picture, a little orange thing was sticking out of the ground, which Ruby assumed was the top of the carrot.

Unfortunately, as she looked around, she couldn't see anything that remotely resembled the picture on her tablet.

"Can anyone here show me a carrot? Be careful if you walk around. Remember, don't step on anything."

Maybe the girls could find them. Clicking back on her notes, she confirmed that "carrot" was on the list of things that Natalie had told her were in the garden.

It was possible, she supposed, that the carrots weren't ready yet. She hadn't thought to ask Natalie about that.

Maybe she should have admitted to Natalie that she had no clue what she was doing in the garden, but she'd thought, *how hard could it be?* After all, she completed some of the most rigorous training known to man, at least intellectually, and became a trauma surgeon. Surely, she could pick out carrots in a garden.

Maybe not. There were some dark green leafy things and some light green leafy things. The dark green leafy things maybe looked like spinach to her. It was already picked and not still on the plant in the grocery store, but the leaves were shaped in a similar way.

"Is this it?" Ava asked, pointing to something in the ground.

Ruby looked over. She looked back at her tablet and brought the carrot page back up. Looking between the plant and the page, she finally shook her head. "I don't think so."

"You mean you don't know?" Ava asked.

She hadn't told the girls that she was an expert gardener, she hadn't even pretended it, but she also hadn't admitted how little she actually knew.

Now seemed like a good time to do that.

"I actually have never been in a garden before. Ever. But we have the internet, and we have our brains, and we can use them both to figure this out."

There. That seemed like a good pep talk. Encouraging them that if they didn't know something, they could always figure it out.

If only.

She bit her lip, then her eyes swept the girls who were staring at her with open mouths.

"I have no idea what any of the stuff is." Pure honesty.

"Some of it might be poisonous. Do you think we could die if we ate the wrong thing?" Rochelle asked.

A good question. One she hadn't even considered. She had assumed they would positively identify things and hadn't worried about it.

What if she ended up feeding the kids weeds?

It was better to be confident, so she said, "No. We're not going to eat anything poisonous. If we have any doubts at all, we'll ask Natalie when she gets back. But in the meantime, do you see how these dark green leaves are planted in rows? You see how they go straight? And now look," she pulled up her iPad where she had searched for spinach, "you see the spinach in this picture? Doesn't that look a lot like what's in the row here?"

She felt like she wasn't teaching them anything, and it was one clueless adult instructing five clueless girls with no one actually learning anything.

Quickly, she typed in the search bar, "how to harvest spinach."

Trauma surgery was her specialty, but in clinical rotations, she'd done enough general surgeries, including bypasses and even several amputations for diabetics, that eating healthy had been something she'd internalized without being taught.

Doctors didn't get much in the way of nutrition instruction, but they saw enough of what bad nutrition did, and she didn't want to be on the other side of the scalpel. Not if she could help it.

So, the idea of a garden was one that appealed to her.

It was not one, however, that she thought was going to be this complicated. She most definitely wasn't going to feel confident enough to weed anything, and even the idea of picking spinach was a little worrisome. What if all those plants weren't spinach? Some of them didn't look the same as the others.

The girls were still bent over, comparing the picture on her iPad to the plants in the ground, when Ruby looked up.

Ethan strode over, the chainsaw in one hand and some kind of box that probably held tools or something in the other.

He looked at home, totally at ease carrying something so dangerous, like he was used to it and it was just an extension of his body.

Maybe it was the way she looked with her scalpel and her scrubs.

She could admire that. Competence in any skill was attractive.

"How's it going?" he asked as he came to the edge of the white picket fence and balanced his chainsaw on the top of it, leaning a little on it and somehow managing to make it look like an act he did every day.

"A little harder than what I thought it was going to be."

She didn't see any point in lying. Although, she had to admit there'd been times in her life where she'd been tempted, and this was one of them. Competence was attractive, incompetence was the opposite. The latter currently defined her.

He grinned. "Looks like you've gotten the internet to help you a little. Any luck?"

"Not much. I assume you planted all this?"

He nodded.

"And you know what we're looking at?"

His grin broadened, and he didn't say anything more but stepped away, setting his chainsaw and the box on the ground before hopping over the fence and making *that* look like something he did every day too.

Annoying in a way, but she also found it hard to take her eyes off him.

Like watching a world-class surgeon do an intricate and complicated surgery. Fascinating.

"Have you figured out you're standing beside the spinach?" he asked. Still grinning.

"We did figure that out. But we weren't sure if the plants in the row were all spinach, or if there were weeds mixed in with them? And will we get poisoned if we eat something that we shouldn't out of here?"

"I don't think there's anything in here that'll kill you, but I wouldn't be sticking random things in my mouth either." His grin hadn't faded; in fact, it might've gotten a little bigger.

But he didn't seem to rub her incompetence in, and she didn't get the feeling he was laughing at her, thankfully.

"If you can become a surgeon, you can master gardening," he said, and his words bolstered her shaken confidence. "But it's really hard to do on your own. I'm impressed." He bent over, pointing at the spinach. "Even though not all of these look the same, they're all spinach plants. Sometimes the leaves on this variety curl, and sometimes they don't. As they get older, they look a little different versus the younger leaves."

He went on to explain to her how to pinch off the leaves and put them in the container she'd brought. He also showed her the other vegetables that were ready, including radishes, peas, and lettuce, and clear over on the far side of the garden, she felt like she'd hit a gold mine when he showed her the strawberries.

"I don't think you'll have any trouble figuring out which of these are ripe. The problem will be keeping everyone from eating them all, so the boys get a few too. Actually, it doesn't hurt to taste them as you're picking though, because sometimes they look like they're ripe, but the very bottom hasn't turned yet. Those will be sour."

Her mouth had started to water, and she could hardly resist reaching down and picking a strawberry off. She'd never eaten one straight out of the garden, and she had a feeling it would be wonderful.

She didn't have to wonder long, because as he was talking, he bent over and pulled a strawberry off, holding it up and showing the girls who had followed them over.

"This one's red the whole way around. The other thing you have to watch for is that there aren't any bugs on it. These aren't like the strawberries that you get in the store. They're out here with all the insects, and while eating a slug or some other kind of insect won't hurt you, it might be a little surprising to crunch down on it in your mouth."

After all she'd been through in medical school and residency, Ruby's stomach was steel, but some of the girls groaned and muttered, "I won't touch that."

Ruby grunted. "Thanks. They're never going to eat strawberries again."

"Hey. I wanted to warn them. What they do with the information is up to them." He handed her the strawberry he was holding. "Try it. I think you might like it. These are Honeyeye strawberries, and they're really good."

Not only did he know what the strawberries looked like, he actually knew what kind of strawberry they were. Again, she stuffed the feeling of incompetence down.

"I know you're going to be fine, so I'm heading out," he said, although he seemed to be waiting.

His eyes flicked to the strawberry in her hand, and she held it out. "You can have it. There's more."

"No. I guess I just wanted to watch you eat it." His words were lower and not laced with the humor that they had been the whole time he'd been there.

Maybe he felt bad that she'd never been in a garden, never eaten a strawberry right off the plant.

She appreciated the fact that he didn't insult her intelligence by telling her she needed to take the green stem off. Even the strawberries she bought at the store needed to be stemmed.

Normally she used a knife, but to her surprise, the strawberry was softer, and the stem peeled right off.

She popped it in her mouth, after a cursory check for bugs, his words still ringing in her ears. She might have a stomach of steel, but that didn't mean she wanted to eat a slug. Even though she knew intellectually it wouldn't hurt her.

The fruit was softer and sweeter, and far more delicious than anything she had ever bought in the store.

"That was amazing," she said, unable to keep the surprise off her face.

He grinned. "The berries in the store are bred to be able to withstand shipping and to stay good for a long period of time.

There's definitely a sacrifice in quality and flavor, and you can't beat these noncommercial varieties right out of the garden."

He didn't wait around for her to say anything more but hopped back over the fence, picked up his chainsaw and box, and sauntered away, whistling.

Chapter Ten

*E*than wasn't sure Ruby had ever been in a garden in her life before. She was game and pretty amazing to jump into something she didn't know anything about.

He admired her grit and determination.

But what he'd really loved was seeing her face as she ate that strawberry. It made him wish there was no camp and no kids and nothing but Ruby and him and that look of surprise and pleasure on her face.

He called over his shoulder, "We'll have a fire going in a couple of hours, and supper can be any time after that."

She waved, acknowledging his words.

Before he turned back, Natalie came down the drive in her SUV. She'd be able to help Ruby in the garden.

Maybe they should have had a better plan, but he always liked to work off the cuff, giving time for what needed it and not being held to a rigid schedule.

That might not work for as many children as they had this year, but he wanted to give it a go before he and Ruby got together and were more stringent.

Unless she wanted a schedule.

Something told him she would work better with a schedule than without.

It was kind of funny to think how opposite they were in that area, which he had never considered before, not that it mattered.

Two hours later, Ruby and all five girls had made it to the campfire.

Ruby sat down in a chair beside him and seemed to wilt, with her head back looking up at the darkening sky.

"Are you okay?" he asked softly, not wanting any of the children to think that there was anything wrong.

"This was much harder than I thought it was going to be."

"Natalie seemed like she was doing okay with you in the garden."

It seemed like she stiffened, and definitely her fingers balled into a fist before she loosened them. As though his words had conjured her up, Natalie's SUV crunched out the driveway.

Ruby glanced over at the taillights that disappeared over the rise. "She was a huge help. But I can't depend on her every day. She wasn't supposed to come back, and she has things of her own to do."

Her eyes closed, and Ethan was so tempted to reach over and, if not rub her back, at least touch her shoulder and let her know that he was there for her.

He didn't. Didn't touch her. Didn't even allow his hand to lift. He couldn't go there.

The kids milled around them, one of the older boys showing the girls that had come how to spray the mountain pie makers, put two pieces of bread in each side, and add filling before putting them over the fire.

"If you think it's going to be too much, we can tell the girls that it's just for this week." Ethan wasn't sure what else to say. He wanted to help her, but ten boys were pretty much his limit. "I wanted to stick around the house some today, and I could have given you a hand maybe, but the cows got out, and that's where we were."

"Maybe I should give you my phone number, so we can stay in

touch a little more, because I was a little worried about you." She opened one eye and looked over at him. "Not that I could have done anything about it. Goodness, I had no idea it was going to be this hard."

"Well, maybe it was harder because you aren't really sure what was going on in the garden."

"So true. I had studied it and thought I would be able to tell a carrot from a beet from spinach, but I really couldn't. I do think I learned some, from you especially, and Natalie was wonderful. You're so lucky to have a woman like her." She closed her eyes and rolled her head back so she looked straight up.

Her comment kind of caught Ethan off guard. Natalie wasn't "his" woman, but that wasn't exactly what she had said. Maybe she was just too tired to know what she was saying.

He sat in his seat and stared at the flames. Sometimes when he didn't know what to say, it was usually best not to say anything.

"Do you have anything planned for this evening?" she asked wearily.

"I'm sorry. I guess I should have gone through the tentative schedule of what I usually do. Typically after the kids eat, and we clean everything up, Dad usually shows up and has a devotional, and sometimes Mom comes and sings with us, and if they don't make it, then I do it myself. Sometimes we play games like charades or flashlight tag. I don't have all the flashlights out though, so no flashlight tag tonight. Once in a while, we play hide and seek. We have to be careful nobody gets hurt."

"That sounds doable. And then bedtime's what? 6:30?"

He laughed. "It can be for you if you want it. Although, you're gonna have to sleep in the living room with the girls. I can make sure the boys all stay up in the hayloft, but there ought to be some kind of adult supervision in the living room."

"I know. I can do this. I survived medical school and residency, I can survive kids' camp for four weeks. Especially if I get weekends off. That's a luxury I'm not used to."

"When I first started, I slept the weekend through."

"Aren't you missing work? Aren't there things you should be doing on the farm?"

"The boys will help me with the things I need to do, like today fixing the fence and getting the cows back in. I've made all the first cutting of hay. I'll start making hay in July after the kids all leave." She looked so tired he couldn't help but say again, "You know it's okay if you don't do the whole month. This is a lot of work."

She didn't say anything for a minute, then she turned her head to look at him. "I'm not giving up. I already have a plan for tomorrow, and I'm working on the rest of the week." She gave a little grin. "This is going to be fun."

His slow grin matched hers. Yeah. That was the Ruby he knew. She just needed a few minutes to regroup and make a plan. And then she'd forge ahead. He bet these girls had no idea what was in store for them, but this would be the best summer camp in the entire state of Arkansas, if not the country. Because Ruby would make sure of it.

BY FRIDAY, Ruby was exhausted. She had no idea how Ethan did this for four weeks straight. By himself.

Natalie had helped her more than she would like to admit. When the boys brought cherries into the kitchen and left with big smiles, Ruby had no clue what to do with them. Thankfully, Natalie helped her make the cherries into delicious pies, and then the next day, they made cobbler, and the next day, they canned what was left.

Ethan had taken the boys with him to give some to their neighbors and then to pass the rest on to Pastor Race to distribute to any parishioners who could use them.

Natalie and Ruby and the girls took pies and cobblers to the neighbor who owned the cherry trees, and that's when Ruby noticed the For Sale sign at the very end of the dirt road.

"Isn't that the farm that you rent from?" she asked Natalie as the girls talked in the back of the SUV.

Natalie nodded, her face serious. "It is. They just put it up Sunday afternoon. Actually, I didn't notice it until I left your place Sunday night." Natalie's hands tightened slightly on the steering wheel, or Ruby wouldn't have thought she was worried about it at all.

"Are they going to let you keep renting if they sell it?"

"I talked to the owner when I delivered the rent check this morning, and he said that it's up to the people who buy it. And who knows when it will sell or who it will be. Sometimes houses are on the market for years. Sometimes they sell in days." Natalie lifted her shoulder. "It's kinda hard not knowing, but this is where faith comes in, I guess. And I've just been trying to roll with it. I don't know what else to do."

Ruby didn't want to pry, but she asked the question that had been on her mind since she had spoken with Ethan earlier that week. "What about your husband?"

Natalie's lips flattened. "He's not interested in us. He's talked to me once since I left eight months ago, and that was to tell me that the woman who moved in with him was taking all of the stuff I didn't take with me to the dump, and he would be serving me papers soon."

Natalie didn't say anything else, and Ruby hated to press the issue. Natalie was such a perpetually happy person, despite her poverty and taking care of the little ones plus helping with the camp. She had to be exhausted every day, but she still showed up every morning with a bright smile, which inspired Ruby, because sometimes Ruby's smile didn't come out until after noon.

"Hey, Miss Ruby, what are we doing this afternoon?" Jasmine called from the very back seat.

"I've a special surprise. I have all of the supplies that I need, and I'm really looking forward to what we're going to do this afternoon." She grinned to herself and couldn't wait. She'd been pathetically inept all week, but today they were going to do something that she felt like she could at least be competent in.

"Are we going swimming in the river?" Maggie asked.

Natalie met her daughter's eyes in the rearview mirror, and Ruby smiled to herself. It was like Natalie was trying to tell her not to ask, but it was too late.

Ruby reached over and put her hand on Natalie's arm. "Don't worry about it. I'm sure everybody wants to know. She was just the one who asked."

She took a breath and turned around. "I was planning on it. It's pretty hot out today. I thought we'd do that after I have my special surprise. Before supper."

"Are we going to like your special surprise?" Haley asked. "Or does it involve a lot of work? Like weeding the garden."

"Is your special surprise that we get to weed the onions instead of the potatoes?" Ava asked suspiciously.

"No. Nothing like that. Just wait for just a bit, and you'll find out."

"Now I'm curious." Natalie grinned.

"You'll just have to wait too." Ruby winked at her. Despite herself, she liked Natalie.

She picked at the material of her jeans and considered whether or not she and Natalie were good enough friends for her to ask the question that nagged at her.

"Ethan's a pretty nice guy," Ruby said casually.

Natalie turned sparkling eyes on her. Then she looked back at the road. "He is."

"And you guys are neighbors."

"We are."

"And..." Ruby decided to just spit it out. "Is there a romance between you two?"

Natalie laughed. "I thought that's what you were hinting at. And you know he's totally head over heels for you. I don't even know how you can ask about that. The poor guy's been mooning over you for years according to your sisters."

Ruby kept trying to close her mouth. It hung open, just kind of swaying in the breeze, but she couldn't quite get it shut. She felt more like a fish flopping on land than a surgeon. Maybe a surgeonfish. That was a thing, right? Although she was definitely more red in the face than blue, despite her lungs working erratically in her chest.

Finally, she found words. "You've talked to Journee and Blakely? They said Ethan likes me?" She didn't know how else to phrase it.

"No. They didn't."

Ruby figured she must have misunderstood. And man, the disappointment ran deep. She looked out the window.

"He's been in love with you since the day he first saw you. Apparently, your family arrived at Race and Penny's and were introduced by the social worker? And apparently Ethan was there?"

Ruby could never forget that day. She could never forget those dark eyes and that silent boy, straight and slim, who stood behind Race and stared at her.

"Yes. That's exactly the way it happened."

"Ever since that day, you're the only one he's wanted."

"But I was going to marry someone else."

"Yeah. From what I heard, he figured until you were married, it was okay for him to want you. I also understand he almost didn't go to your wedding. But he couldn't do that to your parents, which I think was a huge sacrifice on his part. And shows the kind of man he is. He would rather take the pain than give it away. Because the easier thing for him would have been to not be there."

If what Natalie was saying was true, she was absolutely right. But then also, because Ethan had done the right thing, funny how the Lord had worked it out that he was the one whose arms she had run into on the way down the stairs, and she ended up at his house and teaching camp with him.

Crazy how things worked out.

But she had a hard time believing that Ethan had been pining over her all these years. He had a really odd way of showing it, holed up on his farm.

But he hasn't been holed up on his farm the whole time, a small voice said. Every time she'd needed someone, every time she needed encouragement, an ear, a shoulder, a day off, just a little bit of help, Ethan had shown up.

Every time.

He hadn't been there, bugging her when she didn't need anything, and he hadn't asked her—not one time—for anything in return.

But he'd been there.

Chapter Eleven

Ethan had intended at the start of the week to spend a lot more time with Ruby. At least checking up on her and helping.

But she had been pretty much on her own every day until they collapsed around the bonfire each evening. Each evening, he felt like she was struggling. Finally, on Friday, Shane, his youngest brother, had shown up and taken the boys to the woods to grab a load of firewood.

Ethan had two of the boys and planned to mow the grass around the house. He fully intended to check on Ruby while he was there.

He supposed that he should have known Ruby just needed a little time to find her area.

He came around the corner of the house, after putting Kaden on the riding mower, giving Gavin a weed eater, and carrying a weed eater of his own, to see Ruby sitting at the big table with five girls. All of them had cardboard and string and straws and what looked like foam, and a bunch of other craft supplies lay scattered everywhere.

Crafts were a good idea, but he didn't think Ruby would stop at any old craft.

She hadn't seen him, because her back was to him, but her voice was full and confident as she spoke to the girls.

"These bones are called carpals, and as you can see, all four fingers have three, while the thumb only has two. The string that we've attached and threaded through the straws represents tendons. Interestingly, the tendons that attach here are moved by the muscles of the forearm."

She held her arm up and ran her fingers over her forearm as the girls looked at her with their mouths open. Ruby named several muscles, and the girls' eyes glazed over.

Even Ethan laughed himself. She might have been getting just a little deep there.

"And what do you think happens if any of those tendons are severed?"

The girls' eyes were big, and they stared at Ruby.

"For example, if you're cutting something and your knife slips and it goes into your hand like this..." Ruby demonstrated, holding a knife in her right hand and showing it slip and point into her left. "You can sever the tendon in your hand. For example, if it went in here," she tapped with the knife, "you would sever the tendon that connects from your forearm to your thumb, and you wouldn't be able to use your thumb. The restriction of movement would depend on which tendon you severed. Tendons don't fix themselves like skin will. The only way to fix that is surgery, where you attach the ends of the tendon back together. Sometimes finding those ends is quite a chore." She grinned, and the girls continued staring. "Let's see you work your tendons, girls."

Ethan was half amused and half amazed as the girls picked up their hands, each of which had "tendons" running through straws to "bones" that were attached to a foam and cardboard cutout of a hand.

Yeah, he definitely wanted to laugh.

She struggled with the cherry pies and the garden and cooking, and she'd even managed to make his socks look a muddy gray color when she'd had the girls doing the laundry. But of course, she was doing a fantastic science demonstration.

He'd thought she'd put on the best kids' camp in Arkansas. He'd been right. Where else would they have a real surgeon show them the parts of a hand and how they work?

He walked over as the girls chattered among themselves, and Ruby watched, helping when needed.

He couldn't help it, but he leaned over her shoulder and put his lips next to her ear. "I'm impressed."

She about jumped out of her skin, stopping short of a scream, and turned with wide eyes to him.

"Finally. I've been working all week to impress you. It's not easy." She laughed, and the sparkle was back in her eyes, and she looked energized and ready to take on the world.

Man, she was beautiful.

If he were visiting her during her training, this is where he'd leave.

"You've been impressing me all week with your grit and your willingness to learn things you have no idea about. This isn't the first time. It's just the first time I got a chance to tell you."

"You can say what you want, but I'm not believing that for one second. I'm still a failure as a camp teacher or counselor or whatever you want to call me, but today, I finally got it going. I'm pretty excited about next week, because I have a couple ideas for that too."

He looked over at the craft supplies scattered everywhere and the happy faces of the girls around the table. "Should I be scared?"

She lifted a brow and looked a little guilty, which made him think that yeah, maybe he should be scared.

"Nope. You don't need to worry about a thing. Everything is gonna be peachy keen jellybean."

He rolled his eyes and walked away, his heart beating hard and his grin irrepressible.

She was a gem, and for the next three weeks, she was going to be working right beside him.

FRIDAY EVENING, the children left, and it was a little crazy again for a while as they gathered sleeping bags and clothes and made sure everyone left with everything they came with and nothing more.

It was late before the last car pulled out, which happened to be Race taking his load of kids back to Little Rock.

"Would it be better for the kids to stay here for the weekend?" Ruby asked as they stood on the step, waving as the taillights disappeared.

The summer days were long, and the sun hadn't quite set yet.

Ethan put his hands in his pockets. "I suppose they could...even some of them could. We've just never done it that way. Maybe because it was just me, and maybe because I can't imagine having kids and being separated from them for a whole month. Not that young. Even though many of them come from homes where the parents don't care, it just seems like a long time for kids that age."

"You're doing a good thing. And you're probably right, although from talking to a few of the girls, they're definitely better off here than they are at home. A couple of them don't even live with either of their parents. It's sad."

"I know. I was a kid like that. So were you."

"But my parents died. It wasn't like they didn't want me."

"True, there's a difference. When you're not wanted, it has a tendency to do things to you. Especially when it's your parents who don't want you."

"I'm sorry. That was you."

He always seemed so quiet and confident. Capable.

But of course that was him. Of course he wasn't wanted, and she knew it; she just hadn't realized that it probably affected him the same way it affected everyone else. A hurt and pain that a person almost couldn't get over.

Nothing in her training had taught her how to heal that kind of wound.

She supposed psychology was the discipline best suited, but even that she suspected was ineffectual.

It took God to heal a broken heart.

"How's the wedding fallout?" he asked, his gaze settling on her, like he truly cared.

She sat down on the step and looked out at the sunset.

He copied her. She figured he would. She'd noticed that no matter how hard he worked all day, and he did go full tilt with the boys all day long, he liked to idle as the sun was going down. She suspected it was his favorite time of the day, but she had never asked.

"I did actually talk to Wesley...oh, I don't know, maybe Wednesday night after the girls went to bed. He called late, and I think he was drunk." She'd never heard him like that before. But they'd never really had that much free time before, either. "He's in Italy, and he didn't take the florist's assistant, because she was too young. But I think he's met a girl over there. I heard a woman's voice in the background anyway."

"And?"

She looked at her shoulder and crossed her arms over her chest, rubbing her arms against the sudden chill. "He reminded me that if I wasn't with him, I didn't get the benefits of his family and their connections, and he mentioned that the job I was supposed to start at the beginning of September is no longer open for me."

"Whoa. His family has that much power?"

"They do. They're fairly well-known and highly respected. And I would have joined that, and become that, maybe without earning it, at first. Although I had every plan of being just as good as I could be. But yeah, I was taking a job that was open because of his family."

She twisted her tongue and bit down on it. Thinking. What she'd just said didn't sound good. Ethan didn't rush her, and she appreciated that.

Finally, she said, "After our honeymoon, we were going to go to LA and get settled. I assumed I'd be starting in some capacity before my official start date of September first. I'd probably scrub in to surgeries and pick up any slack where I was needed." She blew out a breath. "Not anymore."

"Can you keep your job in Chicago?"

"I'd given them two months of notice, and my last day was a week before the wedding. I might be able to get hired there for something, but I know they hired someone to replace me."

"I see."

He probably did. He'd spent enough time with her over the years to know how things worked.

"Do you need time away from camp for your job search?"

"You know, I've been so driven and so determined to be the best and have the best and do the best, and part of that was to help as many people as I could, and in the back of my head, I guess it's been percolating all week that this was what I needed. This was what was going to happen. I'd be out of a job, needing to find something. And you know, maybe it was some of the things that Dad has said at night with his devotions. I know they're geared to the kids, but they applied to me too. God has a plan for my life. This wasn't an accident. What are the odds that I would have walked in on Wesley and the florist's assistant? I shouldn't have been there. I shouldn't have seen it."

She didn't say, but she also wondered what were the odds that she would have run into Ethan on her way down the stairs and that she would have ended up at his camp.

"You can't think of not being a surgeon. You've spent the last fourteen years learning. You can't just quit."

"No. Never. Being a surgeon is what God made me for. But maybe it's not going to look the way I thought it was going to look."

"That's wise. So you're just going to relax and see what door the Lord opens?"

"I think so. I've never done that before, and it's a little scary, but I haven't had to do anything so far other than walk through the doors when they were opened. And I admit that even after I caught Wesley,

I definitely went back and forth in my head as to whether or not I was going to walk away from him. Isn't that pathetic?"

"Now that I know how your job and your future was at stake? No. That's not pathetic at all. You had your whole life planned out. It wasn't just your marriage that blew up, it was your life and career as well."

She leaned over and hit his shoulder with hers. "That's what I've always liked about you. You get it."

He smiled at her, but it seemed more like a sad smile than anything, and she remembered what Natalie had said.

She wanted to ask him about it, but how do you ask someone that? *Are you in love with me? Have you been in love with me for fifteen years and never said anything?*

Humph. Not likely. Plus, maybe it was true, and maybe Ethan knew as well as she did that nothing could ever come of it. He wanted the kind of woman that she tried to be the first four days of this week and had shown how extremely incompetent she was at it. The cook, the laundress, the person who could make biscuits with one hand and a peach cobbler with the other. Who knew what vegetables to pull out of the garden to make a salad for twenty people for lunch, and who could handle a whole mass of kids running around her while she did it.

"You need someone like Natalie." She hadn't really meant to voice that, but it was true, so why not. That's what he needed.

"I like Natalie. But not like that. She couldn't stand me. We're too much alike."

"It doesn't always have to be opposites attract. An underlying friendship between two similar people makes a marriage stronger than a flaming passion between two opposites."

"I agree." He sighed. "I suppose Natalie and I could make a go of a marriage, and it would turn out okay. I pretty much think anybody could stay married as long as they're both committed to it."

"You know, that's exactly what Wesley and I said. It doesn't have to be a flaming, passionate love affair. Just two people who are committed to sticking together. That's all you need." She was a little shocked that he would even say that. Like he'd read her mind and listened to her and Wesley's conversations.

But then her face fell. "That didn't work out very well for us. I think maybe there needs to be a little something, because after all, I obviously wasn't what he wanted, or he felt like he needed more."

"It was lack of character on his part. Had nothing to do with you." Ethan's words were said with complete confidence.

"You sound so sure of that."

"That's because I am."

She wanted to pursue that and find out exactly what he thought, but on the other hand, she didn't want to talk about it at all.

They'd lapsed into silence for a while before she said, "What's the plan for the weekend? Surely you have some idea of what you want to do?"

"I'd like to take a motorcycle ride tomorrow if you wanted to. It's supposed to be a nice day, and that always relaxes me."

"Is that what you'd do if I weren't here?"

"Probably not." He looked at her sideways, like he was being honest and wasn't sure what she was going to think of it.

"Do I want to know what you'd do if I weren't here?" she asked, only partly joking.

"Work."

She grinned. "I think a motorcycle ride sounds really nice."

Chapter Twelve

It seemed pretty quiet the next morning when Ethan got up and fed the stock by himself. That was always the hardest part about camp, especially after the last day, getting used to the quietness and lack of companionship after the boys left.

He didn't mind being alone and was seldom lonely, but he always fell in love with the boys, thought about them, and worried about them when they were gone.

He didn't rush through the chores, giving Ruby plenty of time to sleep in if she wanted to and to get up and be relaxed.

It was almost lunchtime when he finally went in.

"I was about ready to go looking for you," Ruby said from her seat at the table in front of the window. Her laptop was open, and she had several notebooks and pieces of paper scattered around.

He assumed she was doing whatever it was doctors did to keep up on the latest surgeries and techniques.

So he was surprised when she said, "I've had some ideas for next week. I think I can do better. I'm pretty excited about it."

He put the eggs he'd gathered in a bowl on the counter. "You're really getting into the camp thing."

"How can I not? The girls are so sweet, and you can easily tell all they want is for someone to love them and encourage them and help them. How can I not want to do everything I can to make their lives a little better?"

She didn't really look at him while she was talking but tapped her pen on the table, like she was showing a little more of herself than she was comfortable with and didn't want to have the intimacy of meeting his eyes.

He could understand that. The way he felt about the boys wasn't really something he discussed with too many people. Maybe his dad.

"Well, if you've changed your mind about going somewhere, we don't have to. I just wanted to give you plenty of time to have a relaxing morning and not feel pressured to go running out."

"Thank you," she said, like the idea of him being considerate surprised her. "I did have a nice cup of coffee out on the deck and watched the sun come up. It's beautiful out here. And so relaxing. So much different than the frantic pace I'm used to. It's almost like I have culture shock."

"I think sometimes we live with the throttle wide open, and it's not really the way our bodies were designed. There's always work to do here, but since there's always work to do, there's no rush to try to get everything crammed into one day. You do what you can today and do a little more tomorrow."

"I know that's a smarter way to live. But it's not really the way a trauma surgeon can make a living."

"I figured we could stop and grab something to eat on our way. If you want to, we can eat at a restaurant, or we can pick something up at a convenience store and go to a park. There are some really pretty places in the Ozarks. You probably have some favorites."

"Not really." The tapping continued, and he hoped he wasn't pushing her, but he wanted to ask more.

"Haven't you ever explored the area? You weren't here long after Race and Penny adopted you, but there are some really gorgeous places around, surely you've checked them out?"

"No. I was pretty consumed with studying and doing what I needed to do in order to become a surgeon. I didn't have a lot of money behind me, and while I know Race would have used his influence for me, I figured I just needed to work harder than everybody else. I didn't take too many vacations."

He had a hard time picturing Ruby partying at spring break. Hard, because she didn't seem like the kind of girl that would go, and hard, because he hated the idea of her being there without him.

The spring break scene definitely wasn't his thing.

He shook those thoughts aside. It wasn't any of his business what she did or didn't do, but they were together today, and he considered it his job to make sure she had a good time.

"Consider me your tour guide, and I'll show you some great spots today." It would take the rest of the day, but the stock was well cared for, and he could be gone until after dark with no problem.

"I'm ready to go now." She stood, closing her laptop and then hesitating. "I know I rode the motorcycle here, and I was just so happy to get out of there it didn't even matter, but, I guess I don't really expect you to understand, but in the ER, I've just seen what being on those things can do, and I'm not really comfortable." She set the pen down, very deliberately, perpendicular to her laptop and looked up at him. "I'd rather take your truck if you don't mind."

He looked at her, studying her. It probably wasn't easy for her to criticize his mode of transportation. Maybe she didn't want to be that close to him on the bike, or maybe it truly was what she saw in the ER.

"I...I have the convertible that I bought when we were in high school."

Her head jerked up, and her eyes widened. "You do?" she almost whispered. "I don't know if I ever thanked you for that."

"You didn't need to."

He did that and would have done a whole lot more, but that probably wasn't something he should be saying. Not then, not now, not ever.

He shrugged and started to turn away. It hadn't been his intention to start talking about that.

"High school seems like such a long time ago, and the problems that at the time felt so big look silly now. But after my parents died, and after my family was split up and farmed out to whatever homes could take them, after finally getting everyone together, I just didn't fit in."

She was talking about high school, but she'd been harassed on the streets of town, and that's where he'd really learned about the issues she'd been going through, because she hadn't talked about them at home. The day he'd come upon her coming out of the grocery store with milk and eggs and being teased and made fun of by what he assumed were her classmates as she walked by the park.

He hadn't said anything, but had taken her groceries, and just walked beside her.

The taunting had stopped, but on the ride home, after he put her bicycle on the back of his truck, she'd sat in the cab and told him that the school had thought it would be really funny to vote the socially awkward, new girl that everyone hated onto the homecoming court.

That would be bad enough, but the homecoming committee had decided that everyone on the court would be driven around the track in a convertible, except Ruby didn't have a convertible, and the committee had conveniently only been able to come up with four even though there were five girls.

They had told her she could ride her bicycle.

He doubted whatever adult was overseeing the committee would have allowed that to actually happen, but it had been hurtful and hard, and Ruby had been handling it by herself, because she knew that Race and Penny adopting six kids would be hard enough without her adding to the drama that they would have to deal with.

Plus, she didn't want them to have to spend any money on her.

She'd been going to decline her spot on the homecoming court.

But he'd spent the money that he'd been saving since he was a small child to buy a ranch of his own on a convertible just for Ruby.

They'd gone together. Ironic, because he'd never gone to any of his own dances in high school, but he'd been there that night for Ruby.

"You taught me some things about standing up for myself, about friendship, and about not letting what other people do to me determine how I react. I know I never said anything, but those were lessons that I've used over and over again ever since that day. Not to mention I just appreciated it. It was a big deal for me at the time and still is."

He swallowed and tried twice before he could open his mouth. "It's a big deal for me too." Probably not for the same reasons as her, but it had been one of the best times of his life, even if he'd gone as her "brother."

He supposed they were each deep in their thoughts, and as the seconds ticked by, neither one of them said anything.

She brushed her hands down her legs, and whatever spell had descended was broken.

"Thank you for understanding. I'm ready to go."

ETHAN WAS AN EXCELLENT DRIVER, and he didn't go so fast that she was scared to death, but he didn't putter around either.

Normally she liked to be in control and preferred to drive, but he drove with such confidence that she soon forgot all about it, just enjoyed looking at the scenery which was gorgeous.

After spending so much time in Chicago, the rustic and mostly deserted mountain roads, green with new spring growth and lined with wildflowers blooming in profusion, were as relaxing and enjoyable as the drive itself.

They stopped at a gas station and grabbed some hot dogs and salads for lunch, and as he promised, he took her to an overlook that wasn't exceptionally high but was gorgeous because of the view of the river below, and the rolling hills in the distance, and the endless blue sky with the white puffy clouds which all made for a glorious day.

They sat on a rock, balancing their food in their laps and eating in silence.

It had been loud in the convertible with the wind blowing, and they hadn't done much talking, but she'd been rolling over questions in her head, things she knew she probably didn't deserve to know the answers to and things she probably shouldn't be curious about, but she was.

He knew so much of her past. Maybe not so much her upbringing with her birth parents, although it had been typical in an American dream kind of way, and there wasn't any drama to speak of until her parents had suddenly been taken.

Maybe they were a little different because they homeschooled, and that was probably part of the reason she'd fought so long and so hard to keep her family together.

They'd always been together; just because they lost their parents didn't mean that they wanted to be separated. In fact, quite the opposite. They could have leaned on each other during that time. But they'd been ripped apart almost immediately.

She fingered the hot dog wrapper in her lap. She'd gotten two and only eaten one and hadn't even touched her salad.

Maybe it was Ethan's easy companionship or the gentle laziness of the day, but she glanced over and asked, "What made you start a camp for boys?"

It seemed like an innocent question, not too probing and not too personal.

He didn't answer right away but chewed thoughtfully on one of his hot dogs.

"I guess I just wanted to share what I had."

His answer disappointed her. She'd wanted to know the deeper reasons, although his answer made sense.

"Is there more?" she asked gently, trying not to probe too deeply and willing herself to be content with whatever he said, not pushing for more.

His eyes slid to hers, as though assessing exactly what she meant or maybe trying to figure out if she'd be able to handle what he was going to say.

Surely, he couldn't be afraid that whatever he said would change her opinion of him, but that's kind of the feeling she got.

"I was headed in a pretty bad direction before Race...didn't exactly adopt me, but he definitely took me under his wing. He caught me stealing something from the grocery store. I don't even remember what it was anymore. Instead of grabbing me by the scruff of my neck and calling the cops, he actually allowed me to steal it." He grunted. "He waited for me outside and invited me to his house to eat."

"And a beautiful friendship was born?"

"No. I turned him down. I didn't know at the time that he had seen me steal anything, and I was still hiding it when he cornered me as I came out of the store."

"But then how did you end up under his wing if he let you go?"

"I guess after that, he had his eye on me. He asked around about me, found out that I had run away from home and was basically the scourge of the town. It wasn't a very big town, and as gangs went, I guess I was a gang of one, because I ruled it."

"Why did you run away from home?" She was listening, she really was, and she wanted to know how things worked out with Race, but it just seemed crazy that a child would leave their parents and strike out on their own.

She'd never understood it.

"I lived with my dad and my stepmom. I guess she was a stepmom. She was like the third or fourth woman Dad lived with, although he wasn't married to her. She hated me. Seemed like it anyway." He shrugged. "Eventually, she figured things out, left him, and Dad ended up in prison for what he did to her kids. He'd been doing the same thing to me, but no one stopped him."

Ruby leaned in, staring at the hot dog she'd unwrapped and was getting ready to take a bite out of. She was pretty sure Ethan was saying what she thought he was saying.

Maybe he'd been deliberately vague because he didn't want to be specific. But she had never been very good at making assumptions. She wanted the facts.

So, without looking up, she said softly, "He molested you?"

A warm breeze blew her hair back away from her face, and she lifted her head, feeling the sweet sunshine on her face, seeing all the beauty spread out before her.

They could just hear the splash of the river, and a few late birds tweeted above them. It was so beautiful and so easy to forget that there was death and pain and ugliness in the world.

All she knew about Ethan, the time she'd spent with him, the things she'd heard about him, from her siblings and from Race and Penny, his reputation in the town, anything she'd heard had always been that he was a man of character.

It was hard to believe that something so good could come out of a situation that had been so bad.

But to say she was sorry or to offer some other kind of platitude was probably worthless.

So she simply said, "I didn't know. No wonder you ran away."

"As far as I know, Race is the only one that knows. I might have turned out just like my dad, if it wasn't for Race. I guess I like Race's way better."

"Me too. I love what you've become. Even more so, knowing where you started from."

His fingers tightened on his hot dog, and he looked away. His chest moved in and out deeply. Then, like he was shaking it all off, he lifted the hot dog and took a big bite, chewing in silence.

She picked at her salad, her mind whirling. No wonder he'd chosen to "share what he had." Of course. A lot of those kids were probably in the exact same situation he was, only no one knew it. No one knew it, and he would understand that, because obviously, he'd not told anyone.

There was a fine line there too, she knew. Sometimes kids just got angry at their parents for making them do things they didn't want to. That was part of being a parent, and all too often, it was easy for the children to accuse parents of things they'd never done.

Most of the time, kids knew exactly what would happen to them if they told anyone what their parents were doing. Ruby could sympathize with that too, because she knew what it felt like to have her family ripped away from her, her siblings farmed out anywhere and everywhere, and her parents gone from her life. Of course her situation was different, since her parents were dead, but she could understand keeping quiet and suffering in silence just to keep your family together.

Or maybe because you didn't know any better.

He'd finished the hot dog and balled the paper up in his hand, flexing and unflexing his fingers around it. "I guess I feel like what Race did for me changed my life. I just want to pass it on. I don't know if that'll happen with anyone at the camp or not, but I like to think even if it doesn't, I'm doing something positive in their lives."

His eyes slid over to hers again, dark and deep and holding secrets that she knew she'd probably never hear or find out about, but she understood a little bit more now why.

He eyed her. "I think you probably understand a little bit. Surely, there's some kind of satisfaction in your job, saving lives, changing lives, making life worth living again."

She nodded. She worked with the physical mostly. Although definitely the emotional and spiritual were attached to the physical.

While Ethan worked with the emotional for the most part. And from what she could see with the boys, he did a fine job. As good as any skilled surgeon.

"You're right. I can see the similarities."

"I figured you could." He shifted, putting the garbage in his hand in the bag that sat between them at their feet. "Maybe we can find something a little happier to talk about, so our moods match the day. I wasn't really thinking we'd talk doom and gloom and you'd come back depressed. That's not the goal."

He grinned a little at her. She saw on his face his desire to change the subject and move to something lighter and more fun.

She still had questions, or maybe she just needed to get over her surprise. She hadn't expected him to have a background like that. She kinda figured he came from a poor family, maybe his parents died. She couldn't believe she'd never thought it was as bad as what it was.

They gathered the garbage up, and he said, "There's a trail off to the side here that'll take you down to the river. Or if you'd like, we can drive around some more. There's a bunch more really pretty spots and some neat things to see."

"I get to choose?" she asked with her head tilted, and it felt like maybe she was flirting. Which was weird.

"Yes. Of course. This is your day."

"But you worked just as hard as I did last week." She tried to remember when the last time was that someone catered to just her.

Wesley and she hadn't had that kind of relationship. It was a mutually beneficial, mutually respectful type of thing, where they each assumed the other could take care of themselves.

Someone taking care of her—other than Ethan...it had been before her parents died.

Shockingly, the thought brought tears to her eyes.

She'd gotten over it long ago and wouldn't consider herself sentimental, but for some reason, emotions welled for a moment, maybe because of what they'd been talking about or maybe because of seeing the girls and knowing that could've been her sisters if Race and Penny hadn't stepped up and stepped in.

She'd been seventeen and mostly raised, and even if she ended up in a bad home without her siblings, she probably would have been fine.

Even the short amount of time that they'd been separated and placed into different homes, West had some things happen to him that had changed him forever.

She wasn't even sure what they were. She just knew her innocent little brother had come out of foster care not so innocent and with a whole lot of baggage.

"Let's walk to the river." She lifted her brows as though asking if it was okay with him.

He grinned. "That's what I wanted to do."

Chapter Thirteen

They finished gathering up their stuff. Ethan took it back and put it in the car, putting the top up and locking the doors.

The trail was pleasant, not too steep, and clearly marked. It was unseasonably warm, and by the time they made it to the river, the water looked so cool and inviting Ethan was tempted to take his shoes off and wade in.

Why not?

He sat down on the edge of the bank and started taking his boots off.

"Are you doing what I think you're doing?" Ruby looked at him with half a grin on her face.

"Sure am." He figured it was obvious.

Without another word, she sat down beside him and started taking her shoes off and rolling up her pant legs.

"You know when the last time was that I waded in any body of water?" she asked.

"Come on. You went swimming surely."

She shook her head. "Not since my parents were alive."

"Not even in the ocean? You've not been on LA beaches?"

Her hands stilled as she rolled up her pant leg. "Have you ever been out of Arkansas other than to visit me?"

He shook his head. "No need. Everything I ever wanted is right here." As long as she was there.

"You really should've gone on my honeymoon with me. There's so much more to see than just what you have here."

"That's coming from someone who's never seen this before." He spread his arm out at everything in front of them. "You said yourself you hadn't been around and seen any of the sights. What you've seen so far is pretty good, isn't it?"

"You're right. I had no idea there was so much to see in Arkansas."

"And I haven't seen it all. What's the point in going somewhere else when I haven't exhausted everything here?"

He stood up, brushing his pants off and only half joking. He loved the state and had no desire to be anywhere else, except...

He looked over at her, rolling up her other pant leg and setting her shoes and socks neatly aside.

He supposed, if he had the opportunity to choose between staying here or being with Ruby, he'd choose to stay, but only because he figured she wouldn't be happy with someone like him. Not forever. And he didn't really see any point in doing anything short-term. It was a waste of time.

He didn't feel like he had any life to waste.

Of course, any time he got to spend with Ruby wouldn't be wasted.

She pushed herself up and brushed off. "Deep thoughts?"

He shook them aside. "Too deep for a day like this, that's for sure."

"If this is cold, I'm not doing it." She started walking toward the water, her knees buckling as the stones bit into her feet.

He didn't fare any better. Back when he was a kid, he could run full speed over stones and hot blacktop with the calluses that he got on the bottoms of his feet every summer.

Not anymore. He never went anywhere without his boots on.

"Oh my goodness. It's freezing." She dipped a toe in and jerked it right back out.

"I think the lady is chickening out."

"How about you try it first and we'll see what you do," she said, her hands on her hips.

Ethan determined that his feet would fall off before he jerked them back out of the water, and he took a bold step in, ankle deep. Both feet planted. Throwing a challenging look over his shoulder.

"Feels like warm bathwater to me."

Her lips pressed together, and he could see her tongue working, pushing against her bottom lip as she narrowed her eyes.

"Right." She took a big step and stood beside him, except he'd noticed that the rocks were kind of slippery, and she must've hit an extra smooth one, because her arm shot up, and her other beat the air, like it was clawing for purchase, and one leg came out of the water for balance.

His feet were planted, so he grabbed hold of her arm with one hand and reached over with his other. She grabbed onto his forearm and steadied herself.

"Thank you. You definitely kept me from getting more than my feet wet." She laughed a little and let go of his forearm, but her hand had slid down into his, and somehow his fingers had fitted with hers, and they had become clasped between them.

She didn't pull away, and he didn't let go.

Her eyes dropped to their joined hands, looking at them like she'd never seen hands before. Her fingers were slender in his, but strong, the way he'd expect a surgeon's hands to be. He realized those hands must be very valuable to her. Without them, she couldn't make a living. On the other hand, he could lose a hand. He could lose a whole arm and still farm. He'd known guys who did.

It wasn't a huge risk for her to have her fingers in his, but for some reason, maybe it was the look on her face, he was very aware that he held her livelihood. And she let him.

He hadn't really meant to grab her hand, but now that he held it, he definitely didn't want to let it go. If she pulled her hand away, obviously he wouldn't try to keep it.

But he just couldn't bring himself to drop it.

His blood felt like warm pudding in his veins, and he didn't really want to go deeper into the water. He wanted to take a step closer to Ruby.

But he was pushing the envelope by holding her hand, and he knew it. He shouldn't be. He was just a farmer and would never be anything more.

She was a surgeon, with every chance of being a really good one. Famous. Celebrated and sought after. Not exactly in his league.

His lungs were doing crazy things, and he turned and looked to the other side of the river, trying to take steadying breaths, to talk without embarrassing himself.

He swallowed. "You ready to try walking a little further in?"

"Mmhmm."

Maybe she was having the same trouble talking as he. He highly doubted it. She liked him as a friend okay; he was pretty sure of that. They weren't great friends, that they called each other or even emailed or texted, but when she came home, they talked.

Over the last week, they'd been getting along okay.

"I just realized it's been a week." He looked over at her as they both carefully stepped forward until the water was almost touching their knees. "Are you okay?"

"A week?" Her brows wrinkled, and she kind of tilted her head as she wobbled and used his hand to steady herself. She laughed. "I'm sorry. I can't remember the last time I walked barefoot anywhere, let alone in a river. This is fun." She giggled.

"Me either." He didn't bother to tell her he had been talking about her wedding—it had been a week since her wedding was called off. If she didn't remember, he wasn't going to remind her.

They stopped and just enjoyed the water running over their legs, the sound soothing in their ears. There was something beautiful about the music that water made over rocks, and the scent of the river, the sweet coolness on a warm day.

Of course, all of that paled in comparison to the fact that Ruby was beside him. She'd changed over the years, but that was basically her developing more of the character he'd loved to begin with.

He'd seen the drive and ambition; he'd known she'd possessed it before he'd even laid eyes on her, because she had been the one who had fought to keep her family together. How could he not admire someone like that? And that was still the kind of woman she was.

"I think I could stay here all day. This is gorgeous and soothing like nothing I've been around for a long time."

"I don't have anything else planned," he said, looking down at her.

He wiggled his toes and loved the feel of the water flowing up and over and under his feet.

He wasn't sure exactly what caused it—maybe she'd meant to kick the water with a foot—but one second she was standing beside him, the next second she was flailing and pulling on his hand.

He hadn't been expecting it, although he might've been able to keep her on her feet, except he'd had his foot up at the same time, and when he stuck it back down, it landed on one of the slippery rocks and went right out from under him.

He was pretty sure she would have landed in the water without his help, but he definitely made her end up there a little faster, since he went down before she did.

Their linked hands yanked her down with him.

The water wasn't deep, but they made a pretty big splash as they went down in it, both of them laughing, because what else was there to do? No point in getting upset. Although he hadn't brought extra clothes, and he was pretty sure she hadn't either.

The water wasn't as shockingly cold as he expected, and he didn't pop right back up. Neither did she.

"Are you okay?" he asked as he leaned on his side and looked at her.

"I am. I'd say my pride is bruised, but I'm pretty sure you dragged me down. Although, I'm the one who lost my balance first which threw you off."

"I can take the blame for it. I know I hit the water first. Then I could have let go of your hand, but..." He just hadn't.

Her cheeks glowed, her eyes sparkled, and her hair wasn't completely wet, although it did have darker streaks where it'd gotten splashed.

She was glowing and happy, her smile wide and contagious, and his heart stuttered and lurched. His hand, which had never let go of hers, tightened, and longing pulled through his chest, tight and strong, and he wished with everything he had that being with Ruby wasn't impossible.

Water droplets sparkled on her eyelashes. Ethan lifted his hand up to brush away some of the water that trailed down her cheek, seeing his rough finger against her soft skin, surprised when her eyes fluttered and her lashes rested against her cheek. Maybe him touching her was okay, and he wanted to slide his hand around her chin and push his fingers into her hair, but his hand was wet, and it was Ruby, and nothing could come of this, but he could enjoy being friends with her. He didn't want to make the friendship awkward because he reached for more than he knew he could have.

"Ethan?" she breathed.

"Hmm?" he said, barely daring to move. Not wanting the moment, whatever it was, to end, as the water flowed around them in a world that had shrunk to just Ruby and him. His fingers on her face, her hand clasped in his.

"No one else has ever measured up to you," she said on a soft breath.

So quiet, he almost didn't hear her over the water, and part of him wished he hadn't.

Because her words shot straight to his heart, and it started to race while his mind flew through scenarios...how could it work out?

Was she saying what he thought she was? Could she be serious? What exactly did she mean?

He didn't know what to say. He'd never been great with words, although Ruby had always been easy for him to talk to. Easier to listen to, and easiest to look at. He'd found out in the last few minutes it was not difficult to touch her, either.

"I feel the same way about you," he finally said, deciding to match truth with truth.

Her eyes fluttered open, a little dreamy, but they held an edge of reality. "I have a quarter of a million dollars in medical school loans. I've run over and over in my head how I could move back here, and work at the little hospital in town, and be where I want to be, and be with who I want to be with." The water moved around them as her head moved back and forth. "It's impossible. I wouldn't make enough, even if the hospital would hire me. I just couldn't."

Her lips turned down, and her eyes seemed to beg him to understand.

"You're not meant for a small-town hospital."

Still, he might be able to help her out, to give her more choices for what she wanted.

Another day.

"That's not true."

He watched the water as it swirled between them, not wanting to make assumptions but feeling like she might be thinking the same thing he was. He had to remind himself that she was getting married last weekend.

"Wesley?" he asked softly.

"He's like me. We wanted the same things. I always thought it was silly to go by my feelings." She brought a hand up and put it over his, pressing it against her cheek. "Feelings can be strong, almost overwhelming, and it's hard to fight them, because you're a far better man than he ever was."

"There's no future."

She nodded. "I know."

She pressed her hand tighter and slid her fingers between his, closing her eyes again.

The water flowed continuously around them, and they sat there for a long time.

Not long enough. Not nearly long enough.

Chapter Fourteen

onday morning, Ruby looked at the chickens in front of her. Whole birds. Five of them.

Natalie had brought them Sunday evening and informed her that her youngest child, which Ruby couldn't remember the name of, had a doctor's appointment Monday morning, and Natalie wouldn't be there.

She'd apologized profusely, because Penny wasn't going to be there either, since she and Race had some kind of meeting for the church that they had to go to.

Ruby had told her not to worry about it, that she would take care of cooking the chicken. How hard could it be? To cut a chicken up and fry the pieces?

It would give her something new to occupy her brain with, rather than having it be stuck on Ethan.

They'd eventually climbed out of the river, dried off, sat in the sun on the edge of the riverbank, and laughed about silly things.

They'd driven home with the top up and the heater on as the sun went down, their clasped hands sitting on the seat between them.

They hadn't held hands in church on Sunday, almost by

agreement, but they had yesterday afternoon as they walked together around the farm.

It didn't mean anything. She kept telling herself that. It *couldn't* mean anything.

But she wanted it to.

She had the feeling he did too.

When Natalie had dropped the chicken off, Ruby had been tempted to press her for more details about why she'd said that Ethan was in love with her.

But that was just torturing herself. So she didn't. And now, the girls had been dropped off, and they were all in the kitchen, staring at the five whole chickens sitting on the counter.

Ruby had watched a couple YouTube videos about how to cook chicken, and she had an idea of what she should do, but it seemed a little daunting to have the chickens actually sitting in front of her, and five sets of big eyes staring at her, as she wondered exactly how to start this, how to finish it, and how to have a meal ready for dinnertime.

She wouldn't be overwhelmed, she wouldn't be, and she *would* have a meal ready.

She could do this.

"What's that?" Jasmine poked her finger at the leg of one of the chickens.

"A muscle," Ruby said automatically.

"A muscle?" Jasmine asked.

"Sure. That's the part that you eat—the muscle. It's made up of protein, which your body needs to build muscles of your own, along with your hair, nails, hormones, cartilage, skin, and blood."

She'd probably meant for Ruby to say leg, or drumstick, or whatever, but it was just so ingrained to call it what it was that Ruby had said muscle automatically.

"What's cartilage?" Haley asked.

"Well, funny you should ask." Ruby grabbed her ear. "You have cartilage here." She pointed to her nose. "And here." Dropping her hand, her eye fell on the chicken. "Let me show you what cartilage looks like."

She grabbed the chicken, thankful she'd already made everyone wash their hands.

"This is the skin, which is slightly different than the skin of a person, but the idea is the same. The skin is the largest organ in the body, and it protects you, is your first layer of defense against disease. It also keeps you warm and is where your hair grows out of, which also provides protection and warmth."

She used her knife to cut the chicken's skin off.

"Chickens have feathers, but obviously, we're slightly different than chickens."

The girls laughed, but they were listening too, and so Ruby went on, getting to cartilage, and before she knew it, she was explaining about muscles, then pretty soon each girl had a knife, and she'd shown them the long muscle layers, explaining they were skeletal muscles and showing how they were connected to the bone. She also showed them tendons like they'd made with their straws and strings, and eventually, as she watched carefully, each girl had taken a chicken and time had flown by.

Several hours later, she was barely aware that all five chickens were flayed open on the counter, pieces and parts everywhere, with bones and ligaments, joints and muscles, and she'd been able to show them the chest cavities and how the ribs protected the internal organs and had been launching into an explanation of blood vessels when one of the boys came running into the kitchen.

"Miss Ruby, Miss Ruby! Mr. Ethan told me to come in and get you. You need to come quick!"

This was language that Ruby understood.

How many times had she been woken up in the middle of the night for an emergency, and she went from zero to wide awake, racing down the hall, wondering what she was going to face in the ER?

Immediately adrenaline had started pumping through her body, and she'd taken two steps toward Gavin before she thought to ask, "What's the problem?"

"Jack ran over one of the barn cats with a lawnmower, and it's hurt bad. But somehow Mr. Ethan thinks you can fix it."

Her mind raced. Thankfully, she thought to turn to the girls.

"Girls. Put your knives down and wash your hands." Speaking of which, she needed to wash her own hands.

"Gavin. Run upstairs. There's a purple bag in my room. It's the second door on the right. Go up and get it and bring it down. Hurry."

She was running through her head, trying to remember what all she had in her bag and wondering if there would be anything she could do. Ethan must think there was no time to take it to a vet, or maybe there wasn't one close enough. Growing up, there hadn't been a clinic in town, that she could recall, but she hadn't spent a full year there before she'd gone off to college, so she could be wrong.

Still, it was at least thirty minutes into town. If there was a vet there. If not, it would be longer.

She finished washing her hands and met Gavin as he came down the stairs with her purple bag that contained the medical supplies she took with her everywhere.

"Come on, girls," she called as she started jogging, reaching the door and flying through it, taking the porch steps in one jump, and following Gavin as he led her behind the barn.

Ethan looked up as she approached, his eyes steady and not panicked, but there was a tightness there. Mr. Rogers was a special favorite.

She wasn't used to operating on things quite so small, although she had done pediatric surgery during residency and her internship, too.

"I didn't know if you could help or not. I know he's not going to make it to the clinic." Ethan's voice was calm, but his words were clipped, and she didn't hesitate to drop to her knees beside the prone cat. "Blood was spurting here. I have my finger on it to keep him from bleeding out. I wasn't sure if you could do anything about that or not."

She assessed the cat's condition. One hind leg would need to be amputated no doubt.

The artery Ethan was holding, she could tie off easily. If there were no internal injuries, the cat might make it.

What medicines did she have in her bag? What could she give a cat? Assuming the cat would be about half the size of a baby, dosages would be half of what she had memorized for a newborn.

But she didn't have everything she'd need, like the ability to start an IV, a ventilator, and more medications than any doctor would have in their emergency bag.

But she had enough to give it a shot.

Opening a bag, she grabbed gloves and put them on.

"I'm not sure if I can do this or not, but I'm going to give it my best," she said as she snapped her second glove on.

"I knew you would," Ethan said, his voice soft, some kind of low note in it that caused her eyes to shoot to his. Maybe it was admiration she saw there. Maybe it was just affection, or maybe something a little deeper. She probably looked at him the same way.

Whatever it was, she knew he had the confidence that she would be able to do whatever was necessary, and if it were possible to save the cat, he trusted her to do it.

"Keep your fingers there for just a bit until I spread the tools that I have out, but first I want to put something down, so they're not touching the ground. It's not going to be sterile, but I'd like to keep it as clean as possible."

The children, unusually quiet, had formed a circle around them. She supposed this was probably more educational for them than cutting up the chicken.

Not entirely used to talking while she did surgery but having done it a time or two before with first-year residents, she started, "Mr. Ethan has his fingers pinching off the end of an artery. Girls, that's what you and I were just looking at in the chickens that we were doing."

"I thought you were cooking the chicken?" Ethan interrupted her.

She gave him a baleful gaze. "We got sidetracked."

"Did you just say there's no lunch?"

"Maybe."

Her focus dropped back down to the cat, wishing she had an electric razor to shave the fur. That would have been step number one in the OR, after putting the cat out and hooking it up to an IV. Okay, it would've been about step five.

"We can't have everything. Do you want me to save this cat's life? Or would you rather we stop here and go cook lunch?"

"I thought you had lunch cooking," Ethan said, his finger never lifting from the artery.

"Sorry. We had an anatomy lesson instead." She finished setting the tools out. "Once I finish up here, we'll go back in and cook the chicken, now that we've dissected it."

He snorted. "If you save Mr. Rogers's life, I'll cook the chicken."

"Fair trade," she said shortly, her mind going into surgery mode, picturing the steps that she needed to take. They clicked together in her brain, coming into sharp focus as she picked up a bottle and a needle and said a small prayer.

It'd be really nice if Mr. Rogers didn't die in front of all these children.

ETHAN LEANED a shoulder against the side of the barn, his arms crossed over his chest and his eyes glued on Ruby.

It had been fascinating to watch her.

Two of the girls hadn't wanted to see, and they'd gone for a walk down by the creek. There were three boys who probably wouldn't admit they were grossed out by the mangled mess of the cat's leg, and they were over chopping wood they'd scrounged up from what the loggers had left.

The rest of the kids were gathered around. Ethan had made some of them stand back to give Ruby room and keep from blocking the light, but she'd knelt down on the ground beside the cat, and she'd been amazing.

He had no idea what all she was pulling out of the bag, giving to the cat, and he knew that whatever she was doing was rudimentary at best, but her hands had worked with such surety and confidence, and she'd even given a running commentary the whole time to the children of what she was doing.

She hadn't flinched in taking the rest of the leg bone off, and now Mr. Rogers had a neatly sutured stub where his leg used to be.

Ruby explained to the children what they were going to need to watch for with the cat and what they were going to do with him, which included hot water bottles to keep him from going into shock, and a comfortable bed, and other things that went in one ear and out the other, and he kind of paid attention to it all, but he was far more fascinated and enraptured watching Ruby.

He'd known she was going to medical school, of course. He'd been there at times, helping her. But he hadn't realized how...good... she was.

He hadn't expected this feeling that ballooned inside of him, warming his chest, working its way up his throat to the back of his neck, and he could only term it as pride.

He was proud of his girl.

His brain stumbled.

She wasn't "his" girl.

Maybe part of the feeling that welled up inside of him, that thumped hard with every beat of his heart, that felt like it blossomed and grew...admiration didn't seem strong enough, but he didn't want to use love. He didn't want to love her.

Didn't want to admit to loving her.

Because she was leaving.

And it would hurt.

Her fingers, graceful and sure, gathered up the tools and equipment that she'd used while she gave instructions to the children, getting them to get a comfortable bed ready for Mr. Rogers and a box to put him in, so she could keep him in the kitchen where she could keep an eye on him.

The children scattered to do what she'd asked, and she leaned back on her heels, looking up at him.

She lifted her brows but didn't say anything. He noticed the tightness of her face and the way her eyes were kind of pinched.

He assumed she was tired but maybe also worried that the cat wasn't going to make it. He didn't want to lose Mr. Rogers. He was a favorite.

More than that, he wanted to protect Ruby.

He could read the question in her eyes.

How could he find the words? Even if he wanted to tell her how he felt, he didn't know the words.

"I'm impressed." They sounded so inadequate. He was so far beyond impressed. "I've never seen anything like that."

She smiled a little. "Most people haven't. Maybe it'd be a good thing for everyone to see." She bit her lip and looked away. "Don't be impressed. Mr. Rogers still might not make it."

She didn't need to say that she figured he probably wouldn't. He could read it on her face. He also knew the worry that he saw wasn't necessarily for the cat. It was more for the children and how they would feel.

"Watching you sew Mr. Rogers up was a really good lesson and experience for them." Her lips flattened, and he pushed off from the wall, taking one step and kneeling in front of her. "But if he doesn't make it..." He had to put his hand on her leg, had to touch her.

Her eyes looked at his hand like she'd never seen one before.

He put his other hand on top of hers, knowing that her main concern was not about her skill as a surgeon and personal failure but about the children and how the loss would affect them.

He lowered his voice. "If Mr. Rogers doesn't make it, there's a lesson in that too. It's a hard one, and maybe not one that we want to learn, but still a lesson. And maybe...maybe it would be better for them to go through it while you're here, and I'm here, and we can talk to them about it and help them to see how they can handle it so that if they have to go through the valley of the shadow when we're not there, maybe they'll remember some of the things we say. Not that it makes it easier—death is never easy—we just make it so that they cope better."

She swallowed, loud and harsh. "You're right. I know you're right. But there's a part of me that just can't stand to not have the outcome I want." Her hand slid over top of his, and she lifted her eyes. "Mostly, though, I want the children to see and remember that studying hard and working hard and learning the skills that I just used can save lives. I don't want them to have to face death. Not here. Not when they're supposed to be having fun."

Her eyes begged him to understand, and he thought he did.

"You're saying, beyond the sting of death, that the gardening, the pie making, and the other things that you weren't as good at are important, but you wanted them to see that there are other things that someone can be good at?"

She nodded.

"And maybe, there's a part of you that wants them to see that maybe you do have an area or two that you're competent in." His lips tugged up a little, because he was kind of teasing her, but he also figured he was right.

Her nod confirmed it. That's what he thought.

"Maybe for the children, that's important. But for me, of course I want Mr. Rogers to live. But I don't need him to to know with certainty that you have a gift. It was beautiful and amazing to watch you, and it just confirmed everything I already knew. You were born to do this. It's what God made you for. And there's something unspeakably breathtaking about watching someone do God's plan for their lives."

It was also incredibly sad, because he knew as he was watching her, beyond any shadow of doubt, that there was no way she could move back and give anything up.

She belonged in a hospital operating room, saving lives, working magic, and working hand in hand with God. "And I didn't mean that to take away any of the work that you put into it. Because you couldn't live your purpose if you hadn't worked hard and studied and pushed yourself to become what you are."

For some reason, his words made her eyes fill with tears, and he leaned forward toward her, his hand on her cheek. "Don't cry."

She blinked and swallowed, taking a few seconds before she spoke. "Your words just remind me of something my mother said to me a long time ago, before she died. I'd always wanted to be a doctor. Not necessarily a trauma surgeon, that came later, but I knew the doctor part. And my mom had said that if I was meant to be a doctor, God would equip me with what I needed, but I still had to put the work in and live the struggle." She sighed. "What you just said reminded me of that."

"I guess that sums up life. Work and struggle, interspersed with moments of breathtaking beauty. Like I just saw today." Like he was going through now. Touching her, talking to her, feeling closer to her than he'd ever felt to another human in his life before. It was a moment of incredible beauty that he'd never forget.

"Miss Ruby! Miss Ruby!" Jasmine and Haley came running with the box they'd prepared for Mr. Rogers between them. "We did it just like you said."

"Thank you." She carefully lifted the cat and laid him gently in the box.

"I can carry him in."

"Thank you. I'll gather my things up."

He picked the box up and waited for her while she gathered her stuff and slung her bag over her shoulder.

The two girls who had taken a walk by the creek had heard the commotion and come up. They were already in the house as Ethan walked in the door and set the box down beside it, peering carefully over his shoulder.

Giving them a chance to look, Ethan moved aside as Ruby walked in.

She had put a smile on her face for the girls, the seriousness of the last hour or so gone.

He smiled with her and said to the girls, "He's gonna make it. He'll be the famous cat of camp for the next twenty years."

"Twenty years might be a little optimistic," Ruby said.

He didn't know how long cats lived, but it got a smile out of her. He wished he'd said a hundred years.

She grinned and walked in front of him into the kitchen, going to the sink to wash her hands. He followed her in...and stopped short as he entered.

"Looks like the great chicken massacre happened in my kitchen this morning."

Confusion clouded her gaze as she grabbed a towel to dry her hands, her eyes going from him to the counters as understanding dawned. "It wasn't a massacre. We were dissecting. Did you forget I told you?"

"No. I just didn't believe you."

"Well, there's the evidence."

"I see it. I'm just not sure how I feel about eating it now."

"Why?"

He supposed it didn't matter. She was right. Why would he go all squeamish and not want to eat chicken just because it'd been dissected before he cooked it?

How did he cook it?

"I think stewing it would probably be the best thing to do, but..." He could probably bread the pieces and still fry it. Why not try?

That's what he did, making a breading and explaining to the girls what he was doing, allowing them to dip pieces in the egg mixture and then in the breading and back in the egg and breading before they fried it to a deep golden brown.

It ended up being not half bad. Although he did make a mental note to not give Ruby whole chickens to handle again.

Chapter Fifteen

Unlike the last weekend, they spent that weekend gathering things up to decorate for the Christmas week.

The third week of camp, Ethan had explained, was always spent using every spare minute decorating, and the fourth week was spent enjoying it.

They were in the attic, dragging out huge boxes of stuff labeled "Christmas," when Ruby finally got up the courage to ask, "You must really love Christmas. Since you're going through all of this work to turn your farm into a Christmas wonderland in June, of all months."

Seemed like a lot of work and a lot of heat—the thermometer had been well above eighty all last week—and she wasn't sure how his "Christmas" was going to turn out, because what was Christmas without snow? He'd mentioned something about a snowmaker, but she had trouble believing it could be anything close to the real thing.

Ethan, a ball cap rather than a cowboy hat on his head, wearing a dusty T-shirt and even dustier jeans, with his ever-present work boots on, looked up from the box that he was sliding out of the corner.

In addition to being dirty, the attic was not insulated, and since it was afternoon on Sunday, it was also quite warm.

He hadn't broken a sweat yet though, and she assumed that was because he was used to working outside.

She, on the other hand, could feel her wet armpits and the dribble trickling down her temple.

She was ready to quit, grab a glass of iced tea, and take a shower.

She wouldn't leave him. If he was up here in the heat and the dirt, that's where she'd be too.

Although, she did probably wish maybe once or twice that she could have talked him into going to Italy and Switzerland. The temps there were probably pretty nice right now.

"No. I don't really like all the pomp and circumstance surrounding it. I'm pretty happy just sitting on the porch, spending Christmas Day thinking about where I'd be without it."

Her eyes widened, and she straightened, putting an unconscious hand on the small of her back where her muscles ached.

In surgery, she could move the table up or down and get it in a perfectly comfortable position. She could also adjust the climate control in the operating room so that she was comfortable at all times.

It had a tendency to spoil one.

She waved an arm around, trying to keep the incredulousness out of her voice. "Then what are we doing this for? Surely the kids would rather go swimming, and they love following you around in the woods and cleaning up after the loggers. Do they really want to go through all the work of decorating?"

With the dim lighting, she couldn't be entirely sure of what his face looked like, but he seemed to be thoughtful, maybe remembering something, maybe thinking of the kids.

He shoved a hand in his pocket and leaned an elbow on the big box that sat in front of him.

"You're probably right. About some of them anyway. But I can't do camp in December because of school. A few years ago I did do a camp while they were off on Christmas break. For two weeks." He shifted, and his finger ran along the tape that held the top of the box down. "I think...I think you may be surprised at how many of these kids... They have a Christmas, but there's no meaning behind it. Sometime, there's no family there. I think they all get gifts. I've never heard any of them say they didn't. It's not that. It's not the material things, it's the spirit behind it that they miss." He kinda lifted a big shoulder, not really shrugging but almost like he was giving up trying to explain. But she'd had a light bulb moment while he was talking.

"That's how your Christmas was?"

He hesitated before nodding slowly. "I think most kids are all about the gifts. And that's normal. But what's a little abnormal, maybe, is it's all gifts and no family. No reason, no insight, it's just an empty, shallow, 'me first' mentality. Maybe decorating, and bringing that spirit out, doesn't help anyone, but I like to think it gives them something to think about. Something a little deeper than themselves. Not that they shouldn't be thinking about themselves, because for most of them, if they didn't think about themselves, no one would. But even at that, it's a dangerous thing to start thinking 'I deserve...' Because none of us really 'deserve' anything."

She thought she kind of understood what he was saying. Even though these children were poor and had terrible families, if they were careful, they could still learn, or maybe the only thing they would learn, was "it's all about me. *Life* is all about me."

"And you think Christmas is the best way to teach them that there's more to life than just themselves?"

His face scrunched up, like she had missed his point. "It's not really that. I guess on one hand, some of them really don't get a Christmas. Not like the happiness and the fun and the family feeling, along with the gifts, because gifts are fun. But yeah, it's a good time to think about others...giving away, getting your mind off yourself, using it to think about other people."

She didn't consider that, but he was absolutely right. What

better way to teach kids that it wasn't about themselves than to have them give to others?

"But how do you do that? What are all these decorations for?"

He adjusted his ball cap and looked at the ceiling for a minute.

"Partly for the spirit of things and partly because we invite the church people to come on Friday, and the kids feel like they're giving them something by giving them a special Christmas service in June and by giving them beautiful decorations. The people from church always make a big deal of it, and it's something that both sides look forward to. So it gives the kids a chance to give, and the congregation has been giving the children gifts each year, and often pretty neat things, like a couple families take one kid on vacation with them, and another person takes them to a water park for a day, and a lot of the gifts are just about spending time and doing things with them rather than actual gift gifts, if that makes sense. Taking them on their boat on the lake. Having them over on their farm for a day. Teaching them to make bread. Driving lessons."

She got it now. "The decorations are what the kids do to give. You're teaching them that giving isn't just about money and material things, it's about time, about using what you have to benefit others, and make them smile, and encourage them."

"Exactly. And we do it around a Christmas theme, because that's what God did for us. He gives a gift, but it's not a material thing, it's eternal. And part of giving a gift was his sacrifice. I don't always tie the cross in, but it's there. Because it's necessary. As part of the gift."

She got that. And her eyes were opened a little more to the depth of what Ethan was doing. She thought it was just kind of a fun thing for the kids, and on the surface, it was. But he had so much more he was trying to teach them without coming right out and hitting them over the head with it.

She liked it.

A lot of times, kids learned from example so much better than they learned from any lecture. All they needed to do was look at what Ethan was doing and do what he did.

He'd gone back to moving the box over to the steps where they'd eventually slide it down, along with the other five or six boxes they'd already done, with at least that many more that were still in the back corner of the attic.

She carried the smaller boxes over too. But she hadn't gone back to work and just watched as Ethan, dusty and hot, with so many other things he could be doing, moved boxes of Christmas decorations around so he could teach fifteen kids the true meaning of the Christmas season.

It seemed like a lot of work to go through, but it also showed his heart. As he lived what he was teaching.

Even what she did, her intentions to help people and change their lives through the surgery that she performed, paled in comparison, because she got paid for it.

No one was paying him. The kids didn't pay to come to camp, and no one paid him to put up decorations and spend all this time doing it.

It was a personal sense of satisfaction that he was working for. Or maybe just because it's what he felt the Lord would have him do.

She knew lots of people who had spent years, even more than a decade, learning to do what they planned to spend the rest of their lives doing, but she didn't know any of them who had done it thinking they would never earn a dime.

Not that she looked down on those people—she was one of them —but it made her look at Ethan in a whole new way.

Both of them had things that shaped them in their childhood.

For her, the death of her parents had made her determined to be a trauma surgeon. But she'd never gone into that thinking she wasn't going to make money too.

He, on the other hand, had used the childhood that he'd had— which probably included no Christmas—to do this for the kids, with no thought of payment in return.

He was a true man of character. No wonder she'd dreamed of him from the first.

That wasn't possible; it never had been. But she was honored to call him a friend.

Chapter Sixteen

he next week sped by.

The weeks of camp always did. June would go by so quickly, and he'd wonder where the month went. Race still came out every evening to do devotions with the kids, and they still had a bonfire every night, and the kids still had plenty of time to spend in the river while some of them chose to work during their "time off."

When his hog had a litter of piglets and the runt died, Ruby ended up doing another dissection. Only they didn't have this one for supper.

Being with Ruby would not be a boring life. She'd certainly kept him on his toes during camp.

He'd enjoyed watching her dissection though. The children had had fun as well.

Even the girls who had taken a walk while she was sewing up the cat had watched from the back as she dissected the piglet.

Saturday morning, Ethan held Mr. Rogers as he sat out on the deck porch and watched the sunrise, a cup of coffee in his other hand.

Mr. Rogers had pulled through, surprising Ruby, he was sure.

He wanted to ask her if she wanted to go on another drive that weekend, but all the decorating that hadn't gotten finished during the week needed to be done today, and he didn't have time.

There wasn't a ton, just odds and ends, making sure all the lights worked and that type of thing.

Still, he didn't have an afternoon to give up.

"Deep thoughts?" Ruby asked, coming around the side of the house and startling him.

Mr. Rogers jumped down and landed on the wooden floor with two thumps—front paws hitting together, one back paw hitting.

Ethan watched the feline hop-walk over to Ruby. "I'm impressed with what you did with him."

"I think it was all the praying that I did during surgery, because I don't really know how he survived. I didn't have any of the proper medications."

"Maybe you don't need all that stuff."

She lifted her brows and gave him a look, and he kinda smirked at her. He was teasing. She must've known it, because she grinned back.

Mr. Rogers rubbed against her leg, and she bent down and picked him up.

"We'll be taking those sutures out soon, and he'll be as good as he'll ever be. Definitely not as good as new. Three paws are nowhere near as comfortable looking as four."

"Thankfully he doesn't have to hunt for his dinner. That does kind of take away the stealth mode that he used to have."

Ruby looked at Mr. Rogers, stroking his head. "Can you believe how he's making fun of you? I'm pretty sure it's unkind to make fun of the physically disabled." She shot him a look, which he was tempted to stick his tongue out at, but he didn't.

She was a surgeon after all; she probably did expect some type of decorum out of him.

She walked over to the second chair and sat down. "So, what's on the agenda for today? What are you going to do with your slave labor?" she asked with a heavy dose of humor.

"I'll have her digging ditches and hauling rocks. Of course. And if you're lucky, I might let you take a break and tar the barn roof."

"Think today's a good day to go on strike."

"What? You want me to double your wages? Okay."

She snorted. "My college accounting class was a long time ago, but I'm pretty sure that you could multiply what you're paying me by a thousand, and it would still be zero."

"All I can afford. Now, if I were a big-name surgeon on the other hand..."

"You'd be a quarter of a million dollars in debt and currently jobless. Which is not a good place to be for your mental health and financial security."

She didn't look too worried about it. Maybe she was putting on a good show, but he somehow doubted it. She wasn't the kind of person who pretended.

She'd mentioned it before, but his stomach revolted at owing that kind of money. Even his farm hadn't cost that much.

"It's not cheap to be a doctor. I mean, there's a potential to make a lot of money, but it comes later in your career. People expect, though, that you're rich from the beginning. It's like doctor and rich are synonyms."

"Well, yeah. I agree. Most people do assume that. I did. Aren't there grants or loans or something for that?"

"You know...as hard as I fought for my siblings and me to be together. As badly as I wanted Race and Penny to adopt us. It never even occurred to me that it would screw up my chances to get scholarships and grants. Their income was what I had to put down on any applications, and that pretty much threw me out of consideration for any scholarships and grants. So it was no money all the way, baby."

She lifted a hand and shrugged her shoulder, and he got that. If she wanted to become a surgeon, that was all she could do. He seemed to recall she had a job in college, but the classes she had to take, and the crazy hours that she had in medical school and residency, made any job other than doctoring almost impossible.

"I kinda wanted to go for a ride this afternoon, but we've got too much work to do. We need to make sure all the lights work and all the decorations are up and everything's ready to go, along with a few surprises so the kids have something that will awe them a little bit when they come Monday."

She shook her head. "I can't believe how much work you go through for these kids."

He wanted to brush it off. He didn't want to talk about that. "We have time for a short walk. You want?" His breath caught in his throat as it closed and tightened.

Facing rejection was never easy. Even the rejection of a "no" for a walk.

With a friend. Just a friend.

"I'd love to."

He actually thought she meant that too.

She stood, and he stood beside her. "Nothing fancy. Just on the driveway?"

"Sounds great."

He hesitated for a quarter of a second before he decided that he could take a walk holding his friend's hand.

So, he took her hand, watching her face, questions in his eyes, making sure it was okay with her.

Maybe she wasn't thinking of their time in the water, but he was. Maybe he was thinking that he wished he had kissed her when he had the chance.

They would never end up together, but he really wanted to know what it was like. Even as the intellectual part of his brain insisted that he was better off not knowing. Better off without the memories to haunt him. Or torture him. Still, that didn't change the wanting.

He almost thought he saw the same thing in her eyes, but he was very aware it was exactly what he wanted to see, and a lot of times a person saw what they wanted to.

Maybe their looks said it all, because neither one of them felt the need for words, and they stepped off the porch together, hand in hand, and started up the driveway.

The sun was up, and dew glistened on the grass and on the trees that grew on either side, which were welcome shade in the summer. They'd leafed out and hung down in green profusion.

"You know, the last three weeks here have been some of the best of my life. I love the peace and the relaxation and also the fact there's always something to do."

Ethan wasn't sure whether she was just making conversation or hinting at something more. But he didn't doubt her words were true.

"You've done nothing but work your butt off since you graduated from high school."

"I think that's true for you, too."

"But it's a different kind of work. Like you said, there's no pressure here. Sure, there's work, plenty of it, every day, but it's not life and death." He thought of Mr. Rogers. "Not usually anyway."

"It's too late for me to change my mind about what I'm going to do with my life. And someone needs to do the job that I'm doing. But I love it here."

"You know you're always welcome to come back any time you want. For as long as you want." He wanted to say more. He wanted to ask her what it would take to get her to stay. But he didn't think that was what she was hinting at. She was just complimenting him and maybe saying a little bit of what if.

"I'm sure you would never consider leaving it."

That question did feel open-ended. Like she was fishing. His head jerked around to her. But she walked casually, with no hidden agenda that he could see on her face.

"I never have." That was honest. Would he? He wasn't sure.

They came to the top of the hill, with the driveway stretched out in front of them, maybe for a mile they could see down it and could look over the hill at the sun climbing in the sky.

Neither of them said anything, but they both stopped on the rise.

Her question ran through his head, and he wanted it to mean what he thought it meant, but that skeptical part of him, the part that knew he wasn't good enough for her, told him clearly that she was just making polite conversation. She wasn't asking him to consider leaving nor trying to figure out if he would go with her.

He didn't really mean to, but he turned toward her, and as though her body mirrored his, she did the same until their joined hands linked them and they faced each other on the top of the drive.

He took his free hand and cupped her cheek. She put her hand over top of his, similar to what she'd done in the river, and pressed it closer.

"You remember when you took me to the homecoming dance?"

"Yeah." How could he forget? There hadn't been another girl anywhere that had compared to her that night. "I had the most beautiful girl in the whole school on my arm that night. Not necessarily outward beauty, but the strength of character from inside. I was so proud of you for what you'd done for your siblings. I wanted everyone to know how amazing you were."

His words, sincere as they were, made her lips turn up. "That's funny. Because my thoughts were not nearly so noble. I just wanted you to kiss me."

He choked on his spit and coughed, remembering at the last second to turn his head.

"I'm sorry," she said. "I didn't realize I was going to upset you so badly."

"I just had no idea."

"Then you probably have no idea that I dreamed about your kiss for years. Wishing that I'd had the nerve that night to say something. Then I wouldn't have wondered."

"Isn't it better to wonder than to regret?" He knew it was, had convinced himself it was.

"I don't think so."

"I think it's dangerous. Because we both know this could never work. It's just one of those things that won't."

"I can't argue with you. Because I know that I could never move here. And I wouldn't want you to leave the farm you love and move to me. But as much as I have the head knowledge, I can't convince my heart that you're not the best thing for me. I've never been able to do that."

"Three weeks ago, you were going to marry another man."

"And we had agreed that while we respected each other, we weren't madly in love with each other. I thought at the time I was being smart by using my intellect to choose a husband rather than my emotions." Her fingers ran lightly over his. "And I wouldn't say that it's a good idea to use your emotions solely. Because they're often wrong. Some people love jerks. Maybe, it's best if the two are combined. Regardless, maybe the reason that I had agreed to something like that was because I knew, subconsciously, that unless I had you, that's all I would ever have."

He'd wanted to hear that. Needed to, really. Although it gave him a hope that he knew to be false. Still, she'd shaken his heart and stirred his soul.

Maybe that was just so she could really shock him. Because she said, "Maybe, since I spent so much time regretting the lost opportunity back in high school, we could take advantage of the opportunity we have now."

His eyes searched her face. She was suggesting what he thought she was, he was pretty sure.

It wasn't a good idea. He knew it wasn't a good idea. He was almost positive he was better off not knowing what he was missing. Plus, he'd always had a firm belief that he didn't want to kiss a girl he wasn't serious about. Wasn't fair to her.

But he'd lived long enough to know he probably wouldn't be kissing too many other girls.

If any.

Ruby was always the only one he'd wanted. Any other attempts at any other girls had been half-hearted at best.

Men weren't supposed to be insecure. Confidence was a trait that women admired. He wasn't totally naïve, but he figured he ought to be honest.

"I'm not sure I want to if I'm only getting one chance. I might not be any good at it the first time." His hand slid down her cheek, along the firm edge of her jaw, and back until his fingers wrapped around her neck.

"We've got a week. It doesn't have to be a one-time thing. If the first one isn't any good, we could practice."

His lip lifted, but his heart was so heavy.

He looked away. Back down the driveway at the house where he lived and where, if he were honest with himself, his deepest dream was to have Ruby with him.

"I want to. I want to more than I can tell you. So bad my hands are trembling." He closed his eyes for a moment, like that would make the refusal come easier to his lips. "But what's the point in getting good at it? What's the point of practicing? We both know it doesn't matter how good we get, it doesn't matter how much we practice, it's not like we're married and we have the rest of our lives to practice."

"I've practiced plenty of surgeries I have never had any intention of ever performing again. It was part of my education."

He snorted. Then huffed out a laugh. "Kissing me is part of your education?"

"And yours."

Was she right? He was pretty sure not, but he wanted her to be, wanted it to be okay to kiss the girl of his dreams, even if he knew his intentions toward her could never end where kissing was meant to go.

"I guess I can't turn down the opportunity to further my education, especially when the celebrated trauma surgeon is doing the offering."

He hated the words as they came out of his mouth.

That's not what he wanted their kiss reduced to. Education? That wasn't what he felt. He shook his head. "Forget that. I don't give a flip about education. If I kiss you, that's not why. It's because of... your strength of character, the beauty in your soul, your willingness to fight for the people you love, how you give yourself wholeheartedly, how you take the knocks that life throws you, and you keep getting back up and jumping back in, fighting with everything you have."

His eyes ran over her face as his fingers traced her eyebrow and trailed down her cheekbone. "You're beautiful. I love looking at you. But that's the very least of what I love about you. And it's most definitely not why I want to kiss you. But because of this crazy attraction that has to do with everything I just mentioned and the fact that if you are anywhere around, you pull my body like a magnet. Staying away from you, not touching you, not standing beside you, not having an arm around you is almost more than I can stand. That's why I want to kiss you."

Her eyes had filled with tears, but he couldn't regret anything he'd said. Even if it made her sad, or brought back bad memories, or whatever it was, as much as he hated to see her cry, he couldn't not say the things in his heart. And he couldn't, under any circumstances, let her think he was just kissing her for educational purposes.

"I've never felt this before...the way I feel right now. No one has ever made me feel this way. Thank you. Thank you for being honest with me, for not taking the superficial experience I was offering."

"I wanted to be fair. You have to know that kissing you means everything to me. It's so far from nothing that I can't pretend it is."

"I'm sorry I tried to. Because I feel the same."

He shouldn't kiss her. Even as his head lowered, he knew he shouldn't kiss her when he couldn't offer her any more than a one-week commitment. But telling her how he felt, and knowing she felt the same, made everything different.

How he felt about her, because of what he knew about her, had been the same for years, and it wasn't going to change. He might not be able to have a long-term relationship with her, but he would always want to.

Always.

Their lips met, and she reached up, putting her hand around his neck, pulling him closer. Pressing into her, he caught her sigh, tasted her sadness, and felt the longing for what might have been. Maybe could still be if he could give up his farm and follow her. Maybe he'd do that.

He pulled her closer and ran his hands down her back, his knees shaking, his heart thundering, never wanting their kiss to end.

They both heard the gravel crunching at the same time and pulled back far enough to turn their heads.

He felt the shock go through her and felt the same one in his own body. Seeing the car made him want to jump back, guilty.

"Did you know Mom and Dad were coming today?"

"I had no idea. They've never come to help finish the decorating before, and Race didn't say anything about it last night when he was here for devotions."

"I guess this might be a little awkward to explain to them." She scrunched up her face and eyed him.

"I think I'm gonna be the one taking the hit."

"That's not fair. This was all my idea. You didn't want to." But she didn't deny that their parents would hold him accountable. It's just the way they were.

"I don't regret it. I hope you don't," he murmured. Kissing Ruby in the flesh had been more amazing than any dream he'd ever dreamed.

"Never."

"I kind of was getting into the idea of practicing, maybe later."

She smiled. "I like that. I'll look forward to it."

They turned and, hand in hand, walked toward their parents' car.

Chapter Seventeen

Race and Penny had always been hands-on parents. Even though technically, they didn't adopt Ethan, and Ruby was almost an adult when they adopted her and her siblings, they had taken their parental responsibilities very seriously.

That hadn't changed in the decade and a half that she'd been out of the house.

Ethan had gone to the driver's side where Race was sitting, and Ruby had reluctantly slipped her hand out of his and gone to Penny's side.

Ruby's eyes met Ethan's over the car before Penny's door opened, and Penny gave her a big smile.

"If you don't mind, I'd like to walk with you down to the house, and your dad will drive with Ethan."

Penny had stood and stepped away from the door, wrapping her arms around Ruby and squeezing tight.

Penny's hugs never failed to remind her of her mother's; they felt exactly the same. Delivered with so much love and no judgment.

They stepped back as Ethan stepped around.

Ruby was pretty sure it wasn't an accident that his arm brushed hers before he gave his mother a hug and Penny said they'd talk more once they got to the house.

After the car drew away, Penny linked her arm with Ruby's and started to walk slowly down the drive.

"The first time I came here, before Ethan bought it, he wanted to show it to us to see what we thought. I fell in love with it before we even saw the house. This driveway is so gorgeous, just the most beautiful place ever. I didn't even care what the house looked like. It could have been a falling down, crumbling mass, or a Gothic castle, or nothing." She laughed, the sound sweet and happy in the air.

Ruby's mother had always been in a perpetual good mood. Ruby admired that and Penny, too, and wished she could be like her.

She supposed she'd given herself a pass over the years, when she'd worked thirty-six-hour shifts with barely any sleep. Anybody would be grumpy after that.

Except, she kinda thought Penny wouldn't. Penny had been up for longer, as she sat with mothers in labor and delivered babies, and she'd always come home with a smile. Maybe she was tired, maybe her back hurt, maybe her feet hurt and she was tired of telling some woman she barely knew to just push one more time, but she always, always, always had a smile.

How could Ethan have grown up with that, been around someone like that, and still wanted her? She'd never live up to Penny.

"You're right. The drive is beautiful. But the house is pretty nice too."

"Some people might think it's too old."

"I think it's charming. Sometimes new and improved is good. But I think when it comes to houses, there's definitely character in the old ones."

"I have to agree. Ethan definitely got himself a good one."

Penny was quiet beside her for a few minutes, their footsteps the only sound, before she cleared her throat, rather delicately, and said, "Ethan's been in love with you forever. I was so happy, so very happy, when you came here after finding Wesley. Not," Penny patted her arm with her free hand, meeting Ruby's eyes with a direct gaze, "not that I was happy about what happened on your wedding day. My heart hurt for you, so bad." She laughed kind of humorlessly. "Race found me in the bathroom that night, crying. I was happy that you had gone with Ethan but so torn up about how badly that must have hurt."

"You didn't need to cry, Mom," Ruby said, the word coming to her lips easily. She had two mothers. One that had been killed in a car accident, and one that had adopted her and her siblings when no one else had wanted to take on that much responsibility. "I didn't shed a tear over it. Not one."

Penny sighed. "I'm so happy to hear that. You know, I prayed for years that God would work things out for you...just give you something wonderful, because I knew you deserved it. I didn't think Wesley was that thing, but I didn't want to discourage you, and you hadn't asked me for my opinion."

"I should have." Why hadn't she? Probably because she was egotistical and overconfident and thought she knew what she wanted and didn't want anyone else to tell her differently, except she knew that Penny would always have her best interest at heart.

"Anyway, I'm so glad things have worked out for you two. I've always thought that you two would be perfect together, but Ethan didn't want to get in the way of your education and keep you from being everything you dreamed of."

Ruby didn't say anything. She wasn't sure how to tell her mom that nothing had worked out.

"Some people might look at Ethan and see someone who has no ambition and no drive. By the world's standards, a loser." That made Ruby bristle, but Penny went on. "But there's so much character in him. So much determination to do right. So much upright morality." She nodded absently, a sweet smile on her face. "I'm so glad you could see that. So many people overlook that and underestimate him, when he's chosen that good thing. That thing that's better than anything. Better than success, better than money, better than fame and fortune. I'm so glad you see it."

"I definitely see it. I don't deserve him."

"Oh, Ruby. No! That's not the slightest bit true. You do. And he deserves you. He sees you for what you are. More than the skilled surgeon and the doctor. He sees the character underneath that really matters."

Penny went on for a couple of minutes, and it was interesting, because she said everything that Ethan had just said to her only a few minutes ago. She didn't think anyone else knew that about her, and she probably wouldn't have said it about herself, because she didn't think she was that good. But Ethan had seen it, and Penny had too.

"I'm not expecting to hear wedding bells anytime soon though," Penny said. "Not after what you've just been through."

"I don't think you're ever going to hear wedding bells for Ethan and me. There's just no way."

Penny gasped. "I can't believe that Ethan would be kissing a girl he didn't intend to marry. I know that that's not unheard of anywhere else, but it is kind of unheard of for Ethan. I'm shocked."

"I practically begged him to kiss me, so please don't put that at his feet. But there's just no way we can work it out. He doesn't belong anywhere but on this farm. I can't come here and work in this small-town hospital, even if they did have a place for me, because I have school loans to pay."

The house had come into sight, and Penny slowed down even more. "I know your loans are high. But did you ever think that maybe the Lord's working this out? Maybe you want to be doing what He wants you to do, and let God take care of your med school loans."

"Doesn't that seem a little irresponsible? Shouldn't I worry about paying my bills first?"

"I would never recommend that you not pay your bills. I'm just saying don't be with Ethan unless you're sure that's what God wants for you. And if you are, then don't worry about your med school bills. Bills take care of themselves."

Wow. She couldn't just not pay her bills. She couldn't not worry about them. She couldn't be irresponsible that way.

Was it irresponsible? Or was it faith? She wasn't sure. She hadn't lived by faith. Not much anyway. Sure, she was convinced that being a doctor was what God wanted for her life, and she had faith that everything would work out. Anytime her faith had wavered, Ethan had been there to bolster it.

"Do you think it's God's will for Ethan and I to be together?" she asked hesitantly, because the idea was so foreign. The idea of... trusting God with her love life. With her bills. It felt crazy.

"I think you're the only one that will know that. Other than Ethan. Although, I don't think he'd be with you, if he didn't feel like you were the one that God had for him." Penny took her hand and spread it out, gesturing to emphasize her words. "That's what faith is. It's hard. You can't see the end. That's why it's faith. If it weren't hard, if you didn't have to walk into the unknown, just holding tight to God's hand and having no clue how things were going to turn out, anybody could do it. That's why having faith is such a big deal."

"But God might not work things out the way I want him to." She hated giving up that control. Especially of her life.

Penny laughed. "That's exactly right. It's giving up what you want and just telling God you trust him. That's faith. You trust him, no matter where He takes you, or what He does, or how He works it out. Always assuming that what He does is the right thing and what you wanted wasn't the best for you."

Everything that Penny was saying made sense. Ruby knew it all. She'd been brought up with those thoughts and ideas, but actually putting them into practice?

So much harder.

"God doesn't expect you to have mountain-moving faith today. And you don't need it. All you need is just enough to get you through right now. In the next moment, you'll need faith for that moment.

But God doesn't expect you to have enough faith for the rest of your life right now."

"I might be able to have faith for this moment, but in the next moment, I feel like I'm going to chicken out."

Penny laughed again. "I think God's used to that. Lots of people chicken out. But you've always been different. Out of the billions of people in the world, very few have become trauma surgeons. So you're already doing something that most people can't or haven't. What about this hard thing too?"

Ruby bit her lip and looked at the old farmhouse, the barn, and the newer pole building where most of the Christmas decorations were going up. The trees were up and decorated, there were lights and greenery and tables with toy trains, a giant gingerbread house, and all the other things the kids had put together this week.

All the brainchild of Ethan.

He hadn't mentioned the future. Hadn't mentioned spending their lives together, but she knew Penny was right. He wouldn't have kissed her if he had any intentions of ever being with anyone else.

He probably felt the same way she did—he couldn't ask her to give up her life as a trauma surgeon and live here.

"Just pray about it, honey. I know God will work it out. Just close your eyes and hold on."

Chapter Eighteen

As soon as Ethan got in the car, he felt like he needed to explain to Race what was going on. But the words just wouldn't come.

How was he going to tell the only man who'd ever been a father to him that his intentions toward his daughter were not honorable?

He wanted them to be. But he just didn't see any way that they could.

So he didn't say anything.

They pulled into the house, and Race shut the motor off in the car, but neither one of them moved to get out.

It was probably three full minutes before Race started to talk.

"I was in Ruby's shoes once. After fifteen years of hard work and school and constant learning with sleep deprivation and working my butt off, I'd finally gotten to the point where people were asking me to come and work with them on their team. It's a heady thing. People think you're skilled enough to be an asset to them. People that you love and admire and have admired for years accepting you as one of their own. Such a big deal."

Ethan wouldn't know anything about that. He knew Ruby had

worked hard. And he also knew that Race had been a world-famous surgeon. But all he knew about the education and work it took to get there was what he'd seen the times he'd gone to see her.

"I was so focused on my career, so determined to make a name for myself, that I lost my marriage over it." Race had never taken his hands off the steering wheel, and he tapped it now, just slow taps, like the movement of his hand helped his brain to work. "It's an understandable thing. All that work, all that time, all that effort, all that suffering, you wanted it to pay off and you wanted it to pay off big time. There's a lot of competition too. And no one ever encourages you to slow down. It's always looking for that next hill to climb, the accolades of your peers, their respect and their honor. You don't become a surgeon because you don't want that, crave it."

Ethan didn't really understand that either. For him, his life had never been about himself. Making himself look good. Maybe it was because of his crummy childhood, but he'd never had any problems seeing himself as God saw him, unholy and unclean. Eventually he knew God loved him as a son, but the gratitude from going from the former to the latter had steered his life. There's no way he could live it for himself, not when God had done so much for him.

Although today, he'd definitely been living for himself.

He looked down at his lap and his twisting hands.

"You know Ruby's the same way. She's focused, she's driven—"

"Dad," he interrupted, maybe for the first time in his life. "I'm not pulling her away from her job. Not pulling her away from being a surgeon. I would never do that."

The car was silent.

Ethan felt like his breath echoed in the interior along with his heartbeat.

"I assumed you hadn't. I assumed you couldn't. I was trying to make you feel better."

Ethan turned his head and studied his dad. "You assumed that Ruby and I were just a fling?"

His dad nodded, unsmiling, his eyes studying Ethan. "I did. Am I wrong?"

Ethan dropped his eyes. "No."

"That's my thought. I was just trying to make you feel better. I think, when she gets a little older, she's going to look back at her life and regret what she missed. I know I sure did. Thankfully, your mom and I were able to have a second chance. Maybe you and Ruby will get the same."

Ethan wanted to open the car door and just start to run. Just run until he couldn't run anymore, run until he dropped. Run until he passed out. Just get away and burn up the frustration that writhed inside of him. Race had judged the whole situation with such accuracy it was embarrassing.

"Maybe I could go with her," he said, even though he knew it wouldn't happen. He didn't belong in Ruby's world. He'd be far more out of place than Ruby had been the last three weeks at camp. She'd found a niche for herself and made do with the rest.

He wouldn't be able to do that in the city.

"Penny tried to be with me for a while too. I was too busy for her. Too driven. I neglected her. And you can't neglect your marriage. It will die."

"I don't plan on neglecting anything. In fact, the opposite."

"I didn't say *you*."

"Ruby would never—"

Race put his hand up. "I'm not insulting Ruby. Please. Believe me. I'm just telling you I've been there. I'm telling you how I felt. I didn't see it. I was too young, too driven, too cognizant of the time and effort that I'd put into my education, of the need to make money to pay my bills, to pay back my med school loans, of the need to show the world that I had earned that title of doctor. That I was the best surgeon that I could be. Driven to save lives, not to lose a single one, and every time I did, it just pushed me to be better, to work harder, to study more, to practice more, to know more, so that it would never happen again."

Ethan nodded. He understood. He didn't want to believe it, didn't want to think that was how Ruby felt, but Race would know. And everything that he'd said so far had been right.

"I guess that was a warning then?" Ethan asked, his eyes still on his hands that were folded and clasped tightly in his lap.

"I guess it was. I guess I didn't want to see her hurt you. Not the way I hurt Penny." His breath blew out impatiently. "And I'm not saying anything bad about Ruby. She wants to make a positive difference in the world. Her intentions are honorable. She doesn't even know what will end up happening."

"Then what? What do I do?"

Race pressed his lips together and shook his head. "There's nothing you can do. You're human. The only way I see it working out would be if the Lord does it. I'm sure you've been praying about it. And you just have to trust him to do what's best for you. But you already knew that."

Ethan looked out the window at the barn and the pole building, Slipper and Crimson running around, and thought of the life he'd built here.

It was perfect.

Except he was lonely. Not all the time, and not really something he thought about, just in his heart, he wanted someone beside him. Someone to walk along with him, holding his hand and sharing their lives together. Someone to laugh with and cry with and grow old with.

But not just anyone.

He wanted Ruby.

Chapter Nineteen

*T*he last day of camp was always bittersweet.

On the one hand, at this point in time, Ethan felt like he could sleep for a year and only wake up for coffee.

On the other, it was so hard to watch the kids leave. This year, along with the ten boys and his teen helpers, who had been there off and on, there were five little girls who'd stolen his heart as well.

And a doctor, a surgeon who'd carved it out and taken it for her own.

His eyes landed on Ruby across the hall, standing with the girls and chatting with members of her father's congregation.

The place was crowded, packed really, as it always was. People from the church volunteered to paint faces and bring hot chocolate and make pumpkin pies, although the girls had made pies this year as well.

One lady had brought real whipped cream, and they had a nativity set up, although one chicken had escaped and ran around loose. Any one of the boys could have caught it, probably, but Ethan figured everyone was probably like him and kinda thought it was funny to see the chicken hanging out under the Christmas tree. He'd heard the boys wondering if it was going to lay an egg.

It provided entertainment.

His buddy—a stuntman in Hollywood—who had access to fake snow and a snowmaker, always brought it in, and so little pieces of biodegradable white stuff were floating in the air. It had some kind of crystal type thing in it because it sparkled in the lights.

Christmas music played softly in the background, and the whole place smelled of pine and hot chocolate and cinnamon and spices.

Stepping into the pole building and closing the door, one could easily imagine that it was December, a very warm December, and just about Christmas time.

It was about an hour until Race gave out the gifts.

It was always a drawing. This year, they were separated into gifts that were specifically for boys and ones that were specifically for girls and ones that were for either. That would be new.

It was also new, this hot, tearing sensation in his chest, knowing that Ruby had no more reason to stay.

He'd never gotten those other practice kisses. He hadn't exactly been avoiding her, and they worked well together, but seeing her leave would be harder the more they practiced.

Surely, he was doing her a favor. He didn't want to make things more difficult for her.

This was a summer he would never forget. It was the best camp he'd ever had.

It felt magical tonight, like anything was possible.

Too bad it wasn't.

With God, all things are possible.

He almost laughed at the verse that popped in his head. He believed it. Truly. But some things just weren't meant to be.

He didn't think even God could work out Ruby and him.

You could go with her.

He'd thought of that. He had. But he didn't really think she wanted him.

Why don't you ask her?

They'd kind of talked about it. She'd told him he belonged on the farm. But she hadn't told him that she wouldn't allow him to go with her.

But then he thought about what Race had said. That she would be too consumed with her job and she'd neglect her marriage and family. That, maybe when she was older, she would appreciate it.

He would wait.

He should have asked Race how long. How long it would take until she was mature enough, or old enough, or satisfied enough in her career to want him.

In the back of his head, he assumed he'd be a father someday. He wanted the opportunity to be a better dad than what his own had been. A much better dad.

Maybe that wasn't something the Lord had planned for him either.

Have faith.

Have faith that he would get what he wanted?

Do what you can, and trust the Lord for the rest.

Did that mean that he should do everything he could to get Ruby?

Did he think she was the one that God had for him?

He was almost positive of it. It had been his feeling—what he wanted since he first laid eyes on her.

"Every year, this just gets better and better." Mrs. Weaver, who'd been a member of his father's church for as long as he could remember, put her hand on his arm and tapped it. "What you do for these kids is just amazing. It's so nice of you to let us be a part of it."

"I haven't had a chance to get a piece of your pumpkin pie yet. I hope there's some left for me."

She chuckled. "I have a whole pie set back for you, Ethan. Don't worry about it. Race's oldest daughter, the surgeon, took it to the kitchen when I first got here."

"Her name is Ruby."

"Yeah. I don't know why I can never remember that." Mrs. Weaver's eyes searched the crowd. "Oh, there she is."

Ethan's eyes followed hers, although he knew exactly where Ruby was and what she was doing. She'd moved away from the crowd to the tables that were set up for the gingerbread decorating, and she had the girls from camp, plus a bunch more, all settling down around her.

Ruby had the steadiest hands of anybody he'd ever seen. If anyone could get their gingerbread house to look beautiful, it would be her.

Although, she had a little girl in pigtails who was sitting on her lap and another one with tight curly hair on the other knee. It looked like her gingerbread house was going to be put together by two three-year-olds.

"Looks like she takes after her mother and is good with children," Mrs. Weaver said. "Sometimes those doctor types never marry. So driven with their career, they're just not interested in giving it all up for family. Because you can't have both." Mrs. Weaver shook her head, her expression sad but wise. "You can try, but then you're really burning the candle at both ends. Burnout." Mrs. Weaver twisted her lips. "I didn't spend nearly enough time with my children when they were little. And I didn't spend nearly enough time at my job either."

Ethan listened to her, wondering if this was the Lord's answer for him.

Ruby couldn't do both, and for him to ask her to try was just asking for her to feel like a failure as a wife *and* as a surgeon.

"Well, Ethan, you make your parents proud, boy." Mrs. Weaver tapped his arm again and walked off.

His phone buzzed in his pocket. Pulling it out, he saw it was Joe, who was parked at his house, wanting him to come out so he could give him a check.

Bad timing, but they'd been trying to get together for a while. And Joe was here. He didn't want to put him off.

He stepped out, took care of Joe and was back in in less than fifteen minutes.

The rest of the evening went by in a blur.

The gifts were handed out, children's names were drawn—his mom always took care of it, and somehow she always made sure there was enough for everyone.

His dad gave a brief but pointed message, always able to relate it to the children.

It wasn't quite midnight when things broke up.

It was a shock though to step outside and see that it was still summer and not Christmas outside the building.

Ethan watched and hugged and talked to the few parents who had come to pick up their children. Then he saw the rest of them off as his dad loaded up the van to take them home.

The last of the kids had gotten into the car when he felt someone touch his arm.

Turning, expecting Ruby, he stopped short when he saw Natalie.

Now that he thought about it, he hadn't really seen her much all evening. Although he was sure she was there. He had seen her children. The ones that could walk anyway.

"Have a good night?" he asked.

He looked around for her kids, and like she knew what he was searching for, she said, "They're gathering their stuff up inside. I'm leaving. I just want to congratulate you on a great camp, and I also want to let you know...they found termites in my house and my landlord said they'd most likely be bulldozing it." She twisted her hands together. "I have a month to leave."

His body froze in shock. "You're kidding. Why would he do that?"

Her house wasn't in great shape, but, "Can't they call an exterminator?"

Her face was pinched, but like she was trying to be calm, her voice came out smooth and almost without a tremor. "I don't know. I don't know. All I know is the landlord said there were termites, it was being bulldozed and I'd have to leave." She shrugged, her forehead wrinkled. "Maybe the damage is too bad to save it?"

"What are you going to do?" He was truly concerned. Natalie had been a great neighbor and a huge help with camp, worth far more than the generous amount of money he'd paid her.

Not to mention, he could really relate to her situation. Maybe if his mother had left his father, the things that had happened to him wouldn't have.

Even if they'd lived in worse poverty than what they already did. Probably.

"I don't know. I guess I'll just pray about it. I have thirty days."

They were standing in the doorway, and both of them seemed to have their eyes drawn together to the big old farmhouse sitting across the driveway in the dark. All those bedrooms. Empty.

There were enough for each of her children to have one to themselves, and Natalie, although she was a lot younger than him, could...

No.

Lord, that's not what I want. I'm not going to marry Natalie. I'm not going to take her kids as my own. I don't want that.

He looked down at the dark curls beside him. Her usual bubbly personality and happy smile were missing tonight.

He had the power right now to change that, or at least ease her mind about the future, and offer her peace.

But he couldn't offer to let her live in his house without... marrying her. Could he?

She seemed to gather herself, forcing a smile onto her face and looking up at him. If it didn't reach her eyes, he pretended not to notice.

"Thanks again. Camp is always so much fun. My children look forward to it, and little Jason can't wait for his turn. Next year, he'll be old enough. And don't you think for one second that he's allowed me to forget it all week long." She grinned, the tightness around her eyes and the faint lines on her forehead the only sign that she was about to lose her home and that she had no idea what she was going to do.

She walked in to get her children, but Ethan didn't follow her.

He stood in the doorway, Christmas on one side of him, real life on the other.

He felt there was some symbolism there, but he wasn't sure what it was.

"You know, you could solve her problems."

His head jerked around. Ruby leaned against the building, her eyes on him.

"I wasn't eavesdropping...didn't mean to anyway. I just saw you come out, and I snuck out the back way because I want to tell you what an amazing experience tonight was. It felt so real. After being in there, stepping out into the summer air felt surreal, like summer was the wrong time of year, and Christmas was actually happening."

He stepped away from the door, allowing it to close, and walked to her.

He had every intention of putting his arms around her, pulling her close, but there was something in her stance, maybe the way her arms were a little in front of her, like she was blocking off her space, and he didn't feel welcome.

"Anyway, I think Natalie needs you. You have the power to help her." Ruby's eyes went to his house and looked at it as he had been doing just a few minutes ago. "Can you imagine how happy her children would be to grow up here?"

He didn't say anything.

He'd already been arguing with the Lord. He didn't want Natalie.

"You know, it seems like the Lord plans these things out. And sometimes, it's hard to accept, but you can see how reasonable everything is. How good. How perfectly things fit." She paused, then turned and faced him full-on. "I wasn't planning on having children. Ever. It was something that I figured I would have to give up in order to be a surgeon. I never thought, even for a second, that I could be a good surgeon and a good mother. Maybe some people can. Maybe some people can balance it. But I just knew I couldn't. And look, I don't have to."

"I don't want Natalie."

"I don't want you to have Natalie."

"Then why are you pawning me off on her like I'm a gift basket to be given away?"

"That's not what this is. This is me seeing clearly that that's the way things are meant to work out. I'd wanted a sign. I'd wanted to know for sure. And now I do. Why else would I have come upon you and Natalie and that conversation? You could have had it anywhere, and I would have missed it. But God allowed me to walk in on it and know what needed to be done. I have to walk away. And you and Natalie can make a home here together. It's perfect."

Frustration, panic, fear...they all fought together in his chest, weakening his knees, making his hands shake. He tried to get a handle on his breath.

"Perfect except for one thing. I want to be with you."

"Sometimes what God gives us isn't what we want. It's what we need."

"So this is what you're going to do? You're just gonna leave me for Natalie, just walk away? Just like that?"

Anger had started to win the battle in his chest, and maybe his words came out a little harsher than what he intended.

"Does this look easy to you? Do you think this is what I want? Do you think I stood on your driveway just a couple of days ago and kissed you with my whole heart and soul, and more than that, knowing that you're everything that I want? Everything I love? And every night when I lie down, all I dream about is you? Your kiss. Do you think I want to walk away from that?"

"Then don't."

"I think it's what God wants me to do."

Ethan reached into his pocket and pulled out the check that Rick had given him earlier. "The logger was here this evening. He didn't realize we were having our Christmas festival." He fingered the check. "I talked to him some. And he gave me this."

Her mouth opened and her brows shot up at his abrupt subject change, but she allowed it and went with it. "That's great. I know this whole month you've been expecting a check, and I'm glad you got it. I was a little worried that he wasn't going to pay you. That's great." Her words sounded sincere if not emotional.

"He told me that right now white oak is like gold in the timber industry. I guess they use it to make whiskey barrels, and maybe with the state of the world's economy, or I don't know, but they can't get enough white oak to keep up with the demand for the whiskey barrels. If you have a forest of white oak, it's like you're sitting on a gold mine." He leaned in just a little bit. "That whole two hundred acres they logged off was nothing but white oak."

"That's great. Congratulations."

"Two hundred acres of white oak. I wonder what it's worth?" He fingered the check, his faith growing by the minute.

She shrugged her shoulders. "I'm sorry, I don't know anything about the lumber industry."

"Neither do I. Let's find out together." He unfolded the check and held it so the moon's light shone down, illuminating the writing.

They stared at the number. Ruby gasped just a little bit, but Ethan had a feeling. A faith feeling.

And God hadn't let him down. Not that anything that God did could be a letdown, but he had been sure. He'd been sure since he first laid eyes on Ruby, when she was a seventeen-year-old orphan, he'd been sure that she was the one for him.

He'd never doubted, never strayed, and knew that now God was not changing his mind somehow and all of the sudden wanted him to marry Natalie and fill his house up with her children.

Not that he wouldn't do everything in his power to help Natalie, but he wasn't meant to marry her.

Ruby was the one for him.

"How much are your med school loans?" he asked softly.

"The same as what two hundred acres of white oak is worth. Almost to the penny," she said, looking up into his eyes.

"The first time I laid eyes on you, I knew you were the one for me. There's never been anybody else. Never. The other day, when Race and Penny saw us, and Race talked to me, he explained to me that when he was your age, he wasn't ready for a family, wasn't ready for a wife, he neglected them, neglected Penny the first time they were married because of his career, and he explained how important it was to him. I heard everything he was saying, and all I could think was I've waited for fifteen years, I'll wait fifteen more. I'll wait however long it takes. I'll wait."

She bit her lips and looked away, like she couldn't stand the intensity, or maybe she was just overwhelmed.

"I don't want you to feel pressure. I don't want you to feel like you have to choose me right now. You don't. You don't ever have to choose me. But I know, I know as sure as I'm standing here, as sure as there's a God in heaven, I know he created me for you. And I'll wait until you want me. Because there will never be anyone for me except you."

His palms were sweating, and he had that skin floating sensation that a person gets before they do something really crazy, and he said, "I love you. I have since the first day I met you. And I'll love you until the day I die."

"What about Natalie?" she asked faintly, like her breath had gone out of her and she couldn't get it back.

"It would hardly be fair to marry her when I love you. Would it?"

"I don't know what to say."

"Well, I thought it was obvious, but let me be clear. The check I'm holding in my hand was sent from the Lord to pay for your medical school loans. Regardless of where you decide to go, what you decide to do, I want you to know they're paid off."

"Taxes?"

He shook his head. "Don't worry about them. I'll deal with it. This," he held out the check, "is for you. For your loans."

He thought her chin was trembling, but in the dark, he couldn't be sure. There was no question she took a step closer, then she put her arms around him, and he let her, wrapping his around her, pulling her tight, burying his face in the side of her neck, and breathing deeply. Whatever she decided, he didn't want to forget her scent, her touch, her kiss. He wanted to remember it all.

"Dad's on the board at the hospital in town. I'll talk to him tomorrow and see if there's a position there for me to fill. You...didn't say, exactly, but I was hoping that me being the woman for you and all that means that you'll marry me if I stay."

"Was that a proposal? Did you just ask me to marry you?"

"Maybe. What would be your answer if I did?"

"It's a yes tonight, and a let's do it tomorrow. That's my answer."

She laughed. "I'm good with that."

Epilogue

In church on Sunday, Natalie sat with her children in the back row. She never sat up front with them. Not because they were bad, necessarily, because they really weren't. But because they were kids, and even the best behaved child could be a distraction.

She didn't want to keep anyone from hearing the preaching of God's man.

Not that she was listening.

How could she?

God had given her a place to run to – a place she could afford. One that gave her children a little bit of freedom to play outside, a really great neighbor, and safety from her ex.

Then He ripped it away from her.

She wasn't angry, exactly. A holy God, one who couldn't stand sin, had already given her far more than she ever deserved, paying the penalty for her sin and adopting her as His own.

She couldn't think about that long, because thinking about the depths of that love and the unfathomable scope of that sacrifice would make her cry. Which would worry her children and cause heads to turn in her direction.

They might misunderstand and think she was crying because she was losing her home.

Maybe they'd be half right.

She hadn't come up with any solutions.

Ethan and Ruby sat two rows back from the front — not touching and Ethan's arm wasn't around her, but she bet it would be. If not this week, then soon. Maybe they wanted to wait another week or two, giving the dust from her cancelled wedding time to settle before they announced what Natalie knew to be a soul-mate match.

If it weren't for that, Natalie might be making a desperate offer to her neighbor. Ethan was a good man, and, while she didn't love him, if he weren't in love with Ruby, he probably would have given Natalie a home and possibly a ring, if she'd asked.

She didn't want to have to do that. Didn't want to depend on a man to save her, or for anything, really. She'd been down that road and hated every second of it.

But Ethan wasn't like her ex, and she was fond of him, as she thought he was of her.

Regardless, that was a no-go. She would never do anything to dim the happiness of Ruby and him.

But that left her...out of options.

What could she do that would enable her to keep her kids?

That was all she cared about right now, and she'd do just about anything.

But what?

She thought about the email that she'd sent earlier.

She'd gotten a reply. It wasn't what she'd thought it would be. Wasn't what she was expecting. It probably wasn't a solution, but it might be a distraction. She didn't need that. But, one never knew.

She'd reply to it this afternoon. Who knew what could come of it? It wouldn't hurt to try. She would stop at nothing to keep her children with her and cared for. Nothing.

Join Jessie's list and be the first to know about new releases and sales on her books!

Read Dreaming of His Convenient Kiss, the next book in the Cowboy Mountain Christmas series, featuring Natalie and Denver and the fun marriage of convenience trope, plus one of the best first kisses ever! Keep reading for a sneak peek now.

Sneak Peek of Dreaming of His Convenient Kiss

Natalie Mooney sat at her kitchen table, her divorce papers in front of her.

The children were in bed, and she didn't swipe at the one lone tear that tracked down her cheek.

This wasn't the way she expected her life to turn out.

When she married Eric, she'd never dreamed she'd eventually be sitting at a rickety, Formica-topped, metal table, in a termite-eaten farmhouse, in the foothills of the Ozark Mountains in Arkansas, staring at the paper that was supposed to dissolve five years of her life.

It contained the ashes of her little-girl dreams.

The memories of late nights alone, wondering where he was.

Early mornings the same, only with their children around.

Hospital stays where she farmed her children out to neighbors between contractions, because her husband had to take a business trip.

When she'd questioned him, he'd gotten angry.

It'd taken her years, but when she cleaned out his car, and found the underwear that wasn't hers, and confronted him with it, and he'd denied it at first, but then he let loose with all the things she lacked and all the reasons he needed to find someone else, she'd made up her mind.

He threatened her with physical harm and shoved her into a wall, using his fist on her cheek.

The next time he came home from a business trip, she wasn't there.

Tapping her finger on the table, she looked at the paper and the little perfect circle of wetness that had fallen off her cheek and slowly seeped onto the bottom of it.

Directly beside that, her phone lay on the table, the screen blank.

She didn't need it to be on to know what would pop up when she pressed the button.

Her house was condemned, and she had two weeks left to move.

This place had been dirt cheap. Still, she'd barely been able to afford it with the telemarketing job she did all afternoon and at night after the children went to bed.

She hadn't found another place to compare with the price.

She wasn't being picky. She'd take anything, anything at all that would keep her children with her. All five of them.

That's what had led her to the site that was on her phone now. Marriageofconvenience.com.

It was supposed to be a Christian site, and everyone was supposed to be vetted. She'd put her application in. It had taken her two weeks to be approved, so she thought they were pretty thorough in their vetting.

It was three o'clock in the morning, and she'd spent the last six hours going through the site.

She'd chosen someone.

There were no names on the site—just nicknames—to preserve privacy. When they were both comfortable with each other, they'd reach out to the admins together, and their names would be released to each other. She liked that added bit of security.

The man she'd chosen had included his email address in his

profile—not all of them had—and she felt like she wanted to reach out that way.

She just wasn't sure what to say.

Maybe she should wait until morning when she was more rested, less emotional.

Seeing the finality of her divorce had been more unsettling than she had thought it would be.

Eric didn't have any claim on her heart. Not anymore, and he hadn't for a long time, but it was more that those papers represented the death of everything she'd hoped her life would be and had put her into the ranks of divorcee, had put her children into the ranks of single-parent home, had given her an "ex," and rang with a finality she hadn't expected.

Her body felt painful and numb at the same time. She hadn't known it could do that.

Picking up her phone, she pulled up the mail app and typed in his email address: wilderman@ourmail.com.

The creaks and groans of the little old house didn't bother her at all, nor did the blowing of the wind or the quietness of the kitchen.

Outside, Natalie had to be brave. She had five children watching her.

Inside, she was scared to death.

Her thumbs hovered above her phone. She tried to figure out how best to word her request.

Dear Mr. Wilder Man,

She looked at that. It seemed a little formal for someone she was planning to offer marriage to.

She deleted the "Mr." then put it back in.

His profile said he was a white-collar worker, married once for five years, divorced, and on good terms with the ex. Two children that his wife had custody of, and he had two days of visitation every two weeks. She deliberately looked for someone with a job that didn't include traveling, and his did not. Although he hadn't gone into detail about what he did, just termed it office worker in finance.

She had no idea what that was. Anything from a bank teller to an accountant, she supposed.

Regardless, it sounded appropriately boring and did not involve travel.

Her standards were not high, but she did have them.

She wasn't doing a repeat of Eric. What was the point of living life and making mistakes if one didn't learn from them?

I saw your profile on marriageofconvenience.com. This email is in regards to that.

You can view my profile HERE, but I wanted to tell you a little bit about myself and make my case.

I'm faithful and loyal. I will be completely devoted to you and you alone. I do not need, do not expect, and do not want to be showered with flowers or candy or gifts or any other silly romantic thing.

I've gotten to the point in my life where none of that matters.

Here, she paused, because she was only 23 years old.

Funny how she felt so much older. So. Much. Older.

She'd gotten pregnant at 15, and instead of learning from that mistake, she had another baby before her classmates graduated from high school.

She hadn't. Graduated, that is. She'd had two children.

Water under the bridge.

She was going to learn from that mistake. And every other mistake she made in her life. She was done being stupid.

Probably shouldn't put that in her letter, although she wanted to. *Dear Wilder Man, I'm done being stupid.*

She wasn't exactly selling herself with that.

As she looked back at her phone, her thumbs started moving again.

Your profile said you wanted a traditional wife, and I can assure you that is definitely what I intend to be. I will cook for you, do your laundry, clean your house, I'll even take care of the yard work and vehicle maintenance. You will be well taken care of.

She read that over. Did she sound too eager? It was all true—she wasn't afraid of working, and she wasn't afraid to serve someone else if he was going to provide for her; after all, she didn't even have a high school diploma, so what other kind of job was she going to get —so she left it.

You also said in your profile that you intended to have a real marriage with the intimacies that that entailed. I'm prepared to do that also.

She paused again. That was the one thing she wasn't sure of. It was part of being married, and other than that, his profile was perfect.

She shoved her doubts aside. As long as he was kind to her children, she'd do anything.

As you can see from my profile, I have five children. The only thing I ask in return is that you're kind to them and provide us with basic necessities. Roof, food, and clothes, and I assure you I'm very frugal.

She hadn't had a choice. Getting pregnant at fifteen, when she was too young to hold down any type of full-time job, had definitely taught her to be frugal.

Maybe she should have made some different choices, but it was too late now. Better to not think about them.

She chewed on a fingernail before she added:

I do have a bit of a time constraint. I need to make a decision in two weeks.

She hadn't wanted to come across as desperate, but she felt like she needed to add that last bit, so he knew he couldn't mess around with his response.

I would appreciate an immediate reply, if possible, because of that time issue. I will not contact anyone else for twenty-four hours while I wait to hear from you.

Sincerely,

Mom of Five

Sign up for Jessie's newsletter! Get a free book, access to exclusive bonus content, get fun and funny updates on her life on the farm and more!

A Gift from Jessie

View this code through your smart phone camera to be taken to a page where you can download a FREE ebook when you sign up to get updates from Jessie Gussman! Find out why people say, "Jessie's is the only newsletter I open and read" and "You make my day brighter. Love, love, love reading your newsletters. I don't know where you find time to write books. You are so busy living life. A true blessing." and "I know from now on that I can't be drinking my morning coffee while reading your newsletter – I laughed so hard I sprayed it out all over the table!"

Claim your free book from Jessie!

Escape to more faith-filled romance series by Jessie Gussman!

The Complete Sweet Water, North Dakota Reading Order:

Series One: Sweet Water Ranch Western Cowboy Romance (11 book series)

Series Two: Coming Home to North Dakota (12 book series)

Series Three: Flyboys of Sweet Briar Ranch in North Dakota (13 book series)

Series Four: Sweet View Ranch Western Cowboy Romance (10 book series)

Spinoffs and More! Additional Series You'll Love:

Jessie's First Series: Sweet Haven Farm (4 book series)

Small-Town Romance: The Baxter Boys (5 book series)

Bad-Boy Sweet Romance: Richmond Rebels Sweet Romance (3 book series)

Sweet Water Spinoff: Cowboy Crossing (9 book series)

Small Town Romantic Comedy: Good Grief, Idaho (5 book series)

True Stories from Jessie's Farm: Stories from Jessie Gussman's Newsletter (3 book series)

Reader-Favorite! Sweet Beach Romance: Blueberry Beach (8 book series)

Blueberry Beach Spinoff: Strawberry Sands (10 book series)

From Strawberry Sands to: Raspberry Ridge (12 book series)

Swoonfully Jolly Holiday Stories:

Holiday Romance: Cowboy Mountain Christmas (6 book series)

Cowboy Mountain Christmas Spinoff: A Heartland Cowboy Christmas (9 book series)

New and Much Loved: Mistletoe Meadows (4 books and counting!)

Laughing Through the Snow: Christmas Tree, PA Sweet Romcoms (6 short reads)